WHY WON'T HE LOVE ME?

A Novel By
DENORA BOONE

WHY WON'T HE LOVE ME?

DENORA BOONE

© 2016

Published by Royalty Publishing House

All rights reserved.

This is a work of fiction. Names, characters, businesses, places, events and incidents are either the products of the author's imagination or used in a fictitious manner. Any resemblance to actual persons, living or dead, or actual events is purely coincidental.

Remember….

You haven't read 'til you've read #Royalty

Check us out at
www.royaltypublishinghouse.com

Royalty drops #dopebooks

DENORA BOONE

Acknowledgements

Never will I ever fail to tell God thank you! If it wasn't for Him choosing me to be on this journey, I don't know where I would be. With each book He gives me, He continues to show me my growth in not just writing, but spiritually as well. I still have a lot of growing to do but I know that with Him guiding me I won't fail.

My husband and my best friend, Byron. I know you love me because this writer's life is no joke, and it takes a strong man to love an author! We are moody when we get writer's block, we think our characters are real, and we work serious trap hours. You know all times of night and stuff! Lol!! But you support me and that's big for me. Thank you, baby, for sacrificing to make sure that I'm walking in my calling.

Jalen, Elijah, Mekiyah, and Isaiah, Mommy does this for you! I want to make sure that everything I do now will cause each of you to be more successful than me and Daddy. I pray that God blesses each of you abundantly and that we are here every step of the way.

Charles and Jenica Johnson, what can I say? The two of you are awesome! God used y'all in a tremendous way and I don't know how many times I can thank you for all that you have done. Not just business wise, but in our personal lives. Blood really couldn't make us any closer and I love you!

My AIP family!!!! Boy we may be small but we are powerful, and I thank God for each and every one of you. Every decision I make is to benefit us all. I don't want to leave anyone behind, and as we grow and God sends us more family members, just know that my love will never change. Thank you for believing in me!

Pastor Carlos and Chenille White and my Kingdome Dominion Ministries family, I adore you all. I feel like my family and I have been there forever instead of only a few months, and that's all because of how you welcomed us and loved us. We are so grateful and I pray that everything that your hearts desire, God blesses you with it.

Porscha Sterling and my new Royalty family, thank you for having me. I am blessed to be a part of such a wonderful group of women who wants to see everyone succeed. Regardless of my past, you saw beyond that and opened the door for me. I pray that I can continue to make you proud.

Latisha Smith Burns, sis, you did that! I love and appreciate you just for who you are in my life. You make sure that everyone connected to you is good and in return, I will always do the same for you. Now if we can get you to stop fussing so much then we would be good! Ha!

I know I'm going to forget someone but I promise it's not intentional. But to Deedy Smith, Krystal Sheppard, Deja McCullough, Fanita Moon Pendleton (the best big sis ever), Patrice A'zayler Watts, Yoshi Chance (the best cousin ever), Tanechea Renea Merida, Jade Crystal, and Lorrell 'Plez Her' Wilkerson (the best big brother ever) I thank you all for riding with me like you do. I love y'all so much and each of you have a place in my heart!

To my readers!!! You are the real MVPs, and as long as God gives me I will give you all. I love you!!

Now let's get into this here tea!

-1-

Pulling up to Joe's Crab Shack in Auburn Hills, Kajuana checked herself in the mirror before getting out. The cool breeze hit her face, as she tightened her leather coat around her chest, while holding her purse. She couldn't wait to get inside and get her favorite Tye Dye Swirl in order to calm her nerves. The week that she had been having was like none other, and drinks with her girls was just what she needed.

Kajuana, or Kay as she was referred to by her friends and family, paid no attention to the group of men that were sitting at the bar staring at her when she walked in. Kay could feel their eyes on her as soon as she was seated, and prayed that her friends would hurry up before one of them came over to her.

Her long, dark brown hair fell around her chestnut colored face, and for a BBW, she was gorgeous. Her body may have had a few extra pounds than what society considered normal, but she couldn't have cared less. They were all in the right places and she knew that she could turn heads in any setting. She just wished that her husband Michael saw it that way. This was her reason for needing to meet with her girls.

Before she could get any further in her thoughts, one of the guys from the bar walked over to her and sat down. Looking up into his face, she knew the look she was giving him should have given him a clear indication that she didn't want to be bothered, but he didn't seem fazed one bit.

"You are too gorgeous to be frowning like that," he said trying to strike up a conversation.

No matter how hard she may have tried not to notice, she couldn't help but to admire the chocolate god that sat before her. His jet black hair was really curly, and he had it tapered on the sides. His skin was the color of dark chocolate and just as smooth. He looked to be around six feet tall, which was really short to her for a man, and she could tell by his muscle build that he had to be military. Considering they were in a military town, he just fit the bill.

Kay had yet to say anything to the gentleman, but her face softened a bit as she stared at him.

"Are you guys ready to order?" the little waitress walked up and asked. She was just too bubbly and that irked Kajuana to no end.

"Well for one this isn't my date and two. while I wait on the rest of my party to join me, I'll have the Tye Dye Swirl," Kajuana said before her waitress left to put her drink order in.

"I'm Jason," he said reaching his hand out to shake hers.

"And I'm married," she replied as she held up her left hand to show the ring she had been sporting for the last two years.

Seeing that let Jason know that this wasn't that type of party, and he respectfully nodded his head and got up to walk away. Kay thought it was funny how his boys clowned him once he made it back to his seat at the bar, but she could also see that he was a good sport about it.

Turning her attention back to her phone, she continued to scroll down The Shade Room's Instagram page. She didn't care what was going on with her life, she was going to make sure she was caught up on the latest celebrity gossip. Their drama was kind of like her getaway from her own drama.

The waitress returned with her drink and before she could turn to leave the table good, Kajuana had the straw between her lips as the sweetness of the flavored alcoholic drink cooled her throat and mind simultaneously.

"Look at this lush," she heard beside her and without opening her eyes, she already knew who it was.

"Couldn't even wait on us, huh?" Santana said laughing, as she slid into the booth across from her, followed by Dominique.

The three of them had been friends since their days at Greenbay Elementary in Great Lakes, Illinois. Santana and

Kajuana's fathers and Dominique's uncle, were all in the U.S. Navy and stationed there. From the first day of second grade, they had been joined at the hips and even went to college together.

Santana owned one of the biggest publishing companies there was in the state of Illinois. To date, she had signed over three hundred authors and artists and out of those, over half had gone on to become New York Times Bestsellers. Homegirl was rolling in the dough, but you would never know by just looking at her.

Rocking her hair natural complemented her beautiful dark skin and light eyes. The woman's body was on point and though she wasn't skinny, she wasn't big either. She fell somewhere in between, putting you in the mind of the beautiful and talented Jill Scott. If Kay didn't know her like she did, she would swear they were related in some kind of way.

Tana wasn't big on dressing up. In fact, she hated it so much. The only time she would get jazzy was if she was attending an event, awards ceremony, or a meeting with some investors. Other than that, she was the most comfortable in jeans, a cute shirt, and sneakers. Today she was rocking a cute pair of dark blue jeans, a royal blue V-neck sweater under her leather jacket, and black Michael Kors riding boots.

Dominique dressed depending on the mood she was in. One would guess today she was feeling a little animalistic mixed with a little hood, as she rocked a pair of cheetah print joggers, and some Jordan thirteens that also had cheetah print on them. She must have just gotten them because they looked fresh out the box.

"Okay, you giving us hood Lion King realness with this animal print ensemble." Kajuana tooted up her lips and snapped her fingers before breaking out into laughter.

"Yasss, you already know!" Dominique replied. She was so ratchet but they loved her more than anything.

Nique put you in the mind of Cardi B from *Love and Hip Hop New York*. There were very few times she had a filter on her mouth, and that was only in church. She may have turned up on the outside but as soon as she crossed over into the Lord's house, she toned that thing down. That was their girl though.

Dominique was originally from Brooklyn and her uncle, Javier had gained custody of her after her mother passed. By joining the military, he figured that he had a better chance of being able to raise his niece in a better environment. He didn't feel that New York was the best place for her and he wanted more for his only niece. They moved from base to base before finally being settled in Great Lakes when she was ten.

Just by looking at her, you couldn't tell what nationality she was and although some may have wanted to ask, Dominique's rough around the edges exterior caused them to shut their mouths. Whenever the three of them went out, she was the one that was going to pop off first if someone disrespected her or her girls. Nique had a few more services to attend before she gained the full deliverance she needed from God. Until then, she was just going to be their sister.

"So what you call us here for?" Dominique wanted to know. It was the middle of the week and they normally had their little girls' session every other weekend. It was odd when they received a text from Kajuana earlier in the day, stating she wanted them to meet her here.

Now, it wasn't anything wrong with good food and drinks and Joe's was their favorite spot, but they knew something had to be seriously wrong for her to need them today.

"I think Michael picked his habit of smoking back up," Kay said with tears in her eyes.

Santana immediately moved to sit on the other side of the booth with Kajuana, as she gave Dominique the look she always gave her when Kay thought Michael was back on his weed train. Dominique didn't see anything wrong with it. She felt like it was from the earth so it was all natural. God made it so why not.

Before Santana could stop her, Dominique went in.

"Guh! Ain't nothing wrong with blowing it down every once in awhile. And don't tell me that's not of God while you got that drink in front of you," she said with a knowing look. She loved God just like her friends, but she wasn't crazy enough to pass judgement on one person for their choices because her slate wasn't clean either.

One thing her grandmother always told her was that one sin is no bigger than the next. They all stink to God. Dominique felt like if people would worry about their issues first, they wouldn't have time to be worried about others and classify if they were going to hell or not. It wasn't the next person's place. That's exactly why she lived the way she did now.

She hasn't always made the best choices, and she used to feel so bad when people judged her for having three kids and three baby daddies. To this day, she was unsure of who her baby girl's father was. It wasn't until she started attending Blessed Calvary Church of God in Christ four years ago, that she finally asked God to forgive her and she was able to forgive herself. She still had a way to go, but she wasn't about to let her past determine her future.

"I get what you're saying Nique, but it's more than that," Kajuana said while she used her napkin to wipe her face.

Lifting her head up, she looked around the restaurant trying to avoid her friend's eyes. That was a clear indication that something was really wrong when she wouldn't look them in their eyes. Before turning back to their conversation, she caught Jason's eyes as he looked at her with a face full of concern. Giving him a slight smile, she turned and looked smack dab into Santana and Dominique's smirking faces.

"It's not even like that," Kay said trying her best to sound convincing.

"Mm hmm. But he cute or whatevassss," Dominique said with her tongue sticking out as she raised her hand in the air as the excitement took over.

"We need to look into your family history 'cause I swear you have to be related to Cardi," Santana said laughing at Nique's antics.

"Anyway, what else is Michael doing besides getting kushy?" Dominique asked, waving Santana off and using one of these new phrases for smoking.

"You mean besides draining my bank account, coming in all times of the night, and all of the secret phone calls that he has to take in the other room?" Kajuana asked sarcastically.

"Are you trying to insinuate that he's cheating?" Dominique asked with wide eyes.

"Look at you using big words and stuff," Kajuana said amused. They always joked with Dominique about her grammar. She knew they were joking so she never took it personally.

"You trying to be cute?" Dominique laughed.

"Well, have you talked to him about it?" Santana asked focusing on the subject at hand.

Santana knew how much Michael loved her friend and she just didn't see him stepping out on his marriage. There had to be a reasonable explanation for his behavior but for the life of her, she just couldn't come up with one for him. All of the signs coincided with what Kay was feeling, and had it been her, she honestly would be feeling the same way.

Michael was a good dude and he was good for Kajuana in her opinion. Yeah, he could be a little antisocial with people he didn't know that well, but once he got to know you he treated you like he had known you his whole life. The two of them met their junior year of high school and had been together since. Just like any couple, they had their ups and downs but for the most part, things were good. That was until now.

Instead of answering her with words, Kajuana just shook her head no and reached for her glass. Neither of the women knew what to say because everything that she was saying sounded like the signs of a cheating man.

After a few minutes, Dominique spoke again.

"You know what? The next time he goes out late, we should follow him and see what he's doing. Tana, since Michael is snatching all of Kay's coins, I'm gonna need for you to have some bail money to get me out 'cause if I see another woman, it's going down," she said getting herself hype.

Instead of Santana and Kajuana responding to her, they couldn't help the uncontrollable laughter that followed her statement. Leave it to Dominique to make them feel better when things were looking gloomy in one of their lives.

After talking a few more moments about Kay's situation, they finally ordered their food and caught up on each other's day, before paying their bill and each heading in different directions to their homes.

-2-

Santana woke up the next morning not wanting to get out of her king-sized bed. She had the covers pulled up to her ears as she looked around the dark room. The blackout curtains she had over her windows served their purpose by keeping out the pesky rays of the sun until she was ready to be exposed to it.

Being that Santana was her own boss, she could pretty much set her schedule the way that she wanted it. Checking her schedule for the day on her phone, she was extremely glad that she had completed all of her tasks yesterday and the few things on her to do list could be done from the comfort of her bed.

There were days like this though that she wished she had a husband and children to call her own. She was only twenty-seven and although that wasn't old, she knew that her biological clock was steadily ticking away. The last thing she wanted was to have a baby by the time she was two steps away from a nursing home. That was not the move. Santana wanted to still be full of life so that she could enjoy everything about being a wife and a mother.

Most of the time when men found out what it was she did for a living, they were cool with it. That was until they knew how much money it was that she brought in. When they heard her say she was a publisher, they didn't think too much of it until they found out her net worth was in the millions. Either they were intimidated by her career, or they thought she was so desperate that she would spend all of her money on them. They had her seriously mistaken because she wasn't about to be anyone's 'sugar mama'. Mama didn't raise no fool so as soon as the men showed their true character, she was gone.

The rumbling in her stomach sent a text message to her brain, reminding her that she hadn't eaten since she was with her girls last night. Before getting up to head to the bathroom for her morning shower, she said a quick prayer.

"Lord, I thank you for another day above ground. Let everything I do today bring glory to your name and if there is anything that I have done that was unpleasing in your sight, I ask for forgiveness right now. Have your way in my life and block every attack of the enemy in my life as well as my friends and family. In your son Jesus' name, Amen."

Santana tried her best to not let her feet hit the floor before she thanked God. On the days that she didn't pray, it felt like nothing went right for her. Long ago, she had rededicated her life to Christ and as hard as it was sometimes, she made sure to never let anything or anyone come between her and her father. That's why she had asked God for a godly man instead of a good man. Any man could portray being good, but only one who had a real relationship with God could be godly. A lot of women didn't know the difference, but time and experience had surely opened Santana's eyes.

When she began dating, she thought that if a man took you out and didn't mind spending things on you and letting people know that you were together, that was enough. She started seeing them for who they were, once she became successful and changed her life for the better. That was when she realized and understood the difference.

That godly man was going to make sure he provided for her, but he was also going to make sure that he loved God more than he loved her. He would honor her as his wife, and even before they got married he would show her the qualities of what a husband should be. He would pray for her when she was weak and never be the reason behind any of her tears. Of course, he wouldn't be perfect and would mess up sometimes, but he would never be too haughty to where he couldn't admit his mistakes, apologize, and do everything he could to make sure that he never made that same mistake twice. That was the kind of man she needed and she prayed he would find her soon.

After her morning shower, Santana went into the kitchen to see what she could whip up in order to silence the lion growling in her stomach. She was so hungry that it felt like the pain was in her chest.

Seeing that there was nothing that she had a taste for in her fridge, she decided to throw on something comfortable and head to the nearest IHOP. She could already smell and taste the Banana Foster Brioche French Toast she was going to order along with the extra steak and cheese omelet. Yes God, the anointing was about to be all up and through there.

Grabbing her purse from her dresser and dropping her phone inside of it, she made her way to the front to grab her car keys. Locking the door behind her instead of driving the Mercedes that she usually drove when she went to work, she opted for her favorite ride: her '72 Cutlass sitting on twenty-fours.

She laughed at the thought of how people looked when they saw her sitting behind the wheel. She looked so out of place riding in a tricked out old school car, but it was her favorite. It belonged to her brother Mark before he passed away. It was his most prized possession when he was alive, and she loved it even back then. Riding in it always made her feel like she was right there with him.

Pulling out of her subdivision, she turned on the radio and let the sounds distract her from her thoughts. It had been awhile since her mind drifted to Mark and although she loved her brother, she hated to think about him in his final hours.

Mark was close to ten years older than Santana, so when he died at the tender age of twenty-two, she took it the hardest. Mark may have been older but he was so active in her life. No matter what he was doing, if she wanted to spend time with him he cleared his schedule for her. He would always take her to get ice cream and to the arcade. She knew that he always let her win, but she would still boast about it.

When he was hospitalized unexpectedly and when the test results came back that he had stage four testicular cancer, everyone was shocked. No one knew that he was sick to begin with, so after a month of being in the hospital his body couldn't take it anymore. Her parents took it hard, but not as hard as Santana. She was so distraught that it took her almost a year and a half before the nightmares subsided.

On her sixteenth birthday, instead of buying her a new car her parents decided to give her his. They knew that not only would she take care of it, but it would make her feel closer to him. The days where she had it the roughest, she would either go sit in the car or just ride around, listening to his favorite songs while talking to him. It always seemed to calm her darkest hours.

Finally arriving at the restaurant, Santana whipped into a parking spot, grabbed her purse and hit the alarm on the key fob. Luckily, there wasn't a huge wait considering it was a Friday morning, so there were only a few people ahead of her. When she was finally seated, the waitress asked if she needed a moment before ordering, and Santana let her know that wasn't necessary and placed her order.

As she waited, she decided to send a group text to see what her besties were doing.

Santana: Good morrrnting divas!

Kajuana: Hey boo thang! <3

Dominique: Ahhhhhhhh!

Santana couldn't help but laugh because she could picture Nique with her tongue hanging all out of her mouth being extra.

Santana: You ok today bookie?

Dominique: She better say yeah before I pack up and head out. Y'all know that fighting spirit be jumping on me when it comes to my family!

Santana: Lord why is this girl always ready to fight somebody.

Kajuana: Calm down killa! I'm fine. By the time I got home last night he was knocked out so I just took a shower and went to bed.

Dominique: Oh God must have warned him that it was about to get real in these skreets!

Santana: Nique you so dumb! Got me crying laughing at you and everybody in here looking at me crazy.

Kajuana: Javier must have dropped you on your head when you were little.

Dominique: You tried it!

Santana: Anyway what y'all doing today?

Dominique: I have to be at the shop all weekend. You know everybody trying to get ready to hit the scene this weekend so I gotta go make this paper.

Kajuana: Michael said he wants to spend some time together so I guess I'm chilling with him. Will I see y'all at church tomorrow?

Dominique: I may carry on with some shenanigans but you know I'm beating Jesus to church!

Santana: I wouldn't miss it. Well y'all hit me later if anything changes. Love my sisters!

Kajuana and Dominique: We love you too!

Santana closed out her messages and worked on the few items that she had to get done, right before her food was brought to her. She couldn't wait to dig in, so she closed her eyes to say grace and when she opened them, she looked right into a pair of eyes that seemed to literally ignite something down in her.

This man probably thought she was crazy gawking at him with her mouth slightly opened. She couldn't close it at that moment even if she wanted to. He stood there, never breaking their contact until an older woman on a cane came and slipped her arm through his. That may have been one of the cutest things she had ever seen, as he walked behind their server and helped her sit down.

God had to have sculpted this man Himself and sent him right off the throne in heaven, down to earth. He was about six-feet-three with long neat dreads pulled into an intricate design. His skin was the color of a ginger bread man, and he had some beautiful almond shaped eyes. There was not a lot of facial hair, which was a plus in her book. Santana couldn't smell him but she imagined he smelled like Jesus. Just heavenly.

Lord, forgive me for lusting over this here man! she thought to herself.

The lady that was with him was clearly talking to him and when she noticed he had heard nothing that had come from between her lips, she turned to see what had his attention. At the same time, the two of them blushed and the older woman smiled sweetly and waved in her direction. Embarrassed, Santana quickly waved back and turned her focus back on her food.

Trying her best not to look up as she ate, she tried looking at some new promotional items and creating events for her next few authors' releases. Because she had no one to go home to on the regular, she made God and her job take up even her free time. That was unless she was with her girls.

After eating all that she could, she got her waitress' attention and asked for a to-go box and the check.

"I can get the box but your meal has already been paid for," she told her as she smiled kindly.

Confusion was displayed all over her face so the waitress decided to explain.

"The young man sitting over there with his grandmother already took care of it," she said walking away to go get her box.

Looking up, she noticed Mr. Fine as Wine was looking over at her with a bashful look on his face.

Santana kindly mouthed the words 'thank you' as he nodded his head towards her. After leaving a tip on her table, she gathered her things and headed out to her car.

There was a warm fuzzy feeling that she felt and couldn't remember the last time she felt that way. It had been so long since she had even entertained a man. She tried her best to push the thoughts out of her mind because she knew that she would probably never see him again anyway.

Placing the key into the ignition and turning it, she heard a sound that sounded like an old man choking on cigarette smoke. Santana waited a few seconds before trying it again, only to get the same results.

Santana couldn't think of the last time that she had the car serviced, considering she didn't drive it on the regular, so she figured that had to be it. Popping the trunk from the inside, she got out with her phone in hand and stood in front of the car. It was a time trying to lift that heavy hood and she was relieved when she heard someone say, "Let me get it, sweetheart."

Turning around, she was face to face with Mr. Fine as Wine and just like she thought, he smelled so good. He smelled like nothing she had smelled before on a man, and that made her think of him as one of a kind. It wasn't until she heard him clear his throat that she realized she had her eyes closed, basking in the moment.

"His grandfather used to make me feel the same way baby," his grandmother said with a sly smile on her face. Once again, Santana was embarrassed.

Moving out of the way, she watched him move some things around before asking her when was the last time she got an oil change and a tune up. Noticing it was taking her too long to answer, he knew that it had been a while.

"Go and try to start it now," he said.

Santana did as she was told and as soon as she turned the key, the car came to life. She left it on and got back out as he was closing the hood.

"Thank you so much. How much do I owe you?" she asked reaching into her purse.

He placed his hand on hers and a shiver ran down her back.

Jesus, pick up the mainline 'cause this man 'bout to take me under with just a touch! she said silently to herself.

"That's not needed. I'm glad that I was able to help," he said.

"Ask her to go with you to a picture show or something," his grandma tried whispering but failed miserably. Santana couldn't help but to laugh lightly at the look on his face.

"Really Granny?" he said. Now it was his turn to blush.

He turned to her as he hesitated to speak. He wanted nothing more than to ask her on a date but he didn't even know this woman. Granted, when he walked in the restaurant it was like she was the only one there because his eyes immediately fell on her. He had been observing her for a few moments before she looked up at him. It was in that moment he didn't know what it was about her, but he wanted to get to know her more.

The whole time he ate, he would steal quick glances at her, all the while his grandmother Hattie was trying to talk to him about an upcoming conference her church was having. It was so hard for him to pay attention to her and he kept apologizing for missing the things she said.

"Would you accompany me to a movie sometime?" he asked her.

"Nope," Santana said with a straight face before she continued. "I can't go somewhere with a man that I don't even know his name and he doesn't know mine."

"You are absolutely right. I'm Cortez and this lovely lady is my grandmother Hattie," he said.

"Nice to meet you both Ms. Hattie and Cortez, I'm Santana," she said smiling at the older woman.

"That's such a pretty name but you can call me Granny." Santana smiled without saying a word, as she focused back on Mr. Fine as Wine. Since she now knew his name, she would call him that out loud but in her head, his nickname would stay.

"So can we do dinner and a movie?" Cortez asked now that the introductions were done.

"No," Santana said as she laughed on the inside. She wondered if he would do the typical man thing when a woman rejected them by calling her out of her name and storming off. When he didn't, she was surprised. The next thing she said would determine if she would go out with him or not. Usually, when she asked men to do this they either lied about coming and didn't show, or would just stop talking to her altogether.

Cortez stood there like he was waiting on her to explain herself, but he didn't look upset. He looked more hurt than anything, so she decided to put him out of his misery.

"No we can't go to dinner and a movie, but if you want to spend time with me how about you meet me for Sunday worship service and then we can grab lunch after," Santana suggested, and immediately waited for his response.

She noticed that Granny looked very pleased with her suggestion and she, too, waited for what he would say.

"What church and what time?" he wanted to know, shocking Santana. You could have knocked her over with a feather when he gave her answer.

"Blessed Calvary and ten o'clock." She was sure the look on her face showed that she was pleasantly surprised by his answer.

Cortez was shocked that she asked him to go to church. His experience in the dating world had never produced a woman that wanted to go to church, let alone ask him for their first date to be at one. Something about this change from what he was used to had him wanting to get to know more about the beautiful woman before him. He had always been taught that when God presented him his wife, he would know. The feeling fluttering around inside of him was one that he had never experienced before, and he was curious to see where it would go.

After exchanging numbers, they all parted ways and Santana couldn't help the smile that was plastered on her face. She was hoping that this would be the beginning of something that was meaningful because she wasn't in the game for just casualties. It was time for her to settle down and she wanted a man that was ready to take the same step that she was. All she had asked for that if it was God's will that it be done, concerning Mr. Fine as Wine.

-3-

It was only a little after nine when Dominique walked into her shop 'Styled by Nique' and it was already jumping with patrons ready to get their hair laid. Her first appointment wasn't for another hour, so she had time to go over her books and make sure her stylists had everything they needed.

Dominique may have been a little hood but she was definitely about her business. Her uncle Javier made sure after her mother passed away, that she was well taken care of. He would do anything for her and that's why she worked so hard to show him that his hard work wasn't in vain. At least not all of it.

Her business may have been on point, but her personal life was a hot mess. She had gotten into so much dealing with men that her uncle didn't know what to do. When she got pregnant with her first son, KJ at the age of sixteen, and then Julian when KJ was only six months old, Dominique thought for sure he was going to strangle her. Instead, he loved her through her mistakes and helped her in any way he could. The only thing he provided was a roof and occasional babysitting but other than that, Dominique faced her responsibilities like an adult should.

When she moved out right after her twenty-first birthday into her own house, that's when she started to get a little out of control. It was like as long as she was under her uncle's roof she tried to maintain following the rules, but as soon as she was on her own the turn up began.

Every weekend she was partying and in somebody's club, and no matter how much Santana and Kajuana begged her to stop living the wild life, it was just too much fun to let go.

She always said that when people in the church said they didn't have fun when they were out there sinning, and being saved was the best time they have ever had, she immediately knew they were putting on. The best time she ever had was when she was out there wilding out and doing what she wanted. Dominique lived without limits and not having those limits cost her something that she never wanted to give away.

The night she was raped had been the night to change her life forever. It was her wakeup call when she woke up in the hospital with bandages around her head and her uncle and his wife, Sephora sitting by her bedside crying. When she was finally alert, they reminded her of what had happened and even told her that she was thirteen weeks pregnant. She had no idea she was carrying another baby. One thing she was glad of was the fact that she knew for sure she wasn't carrying the baby of a rapist, but that thought was soon washed away when she remembered that she didn't know who this baby's father even was.

If it had been the rapist, at least she would know where the baby was conceived but because of her wild ways, she didn't know. Even after her daughter, Quatrice was born, she couldn't tell who she looked like. Her skin was a few shades darker than Dominique's but other than that difference, her daughter was the spitting image of her.

It was on her hospital bed that she got saved two years ago and no matter what, she didn't want to go back to that lifestyle. She still had a little reputation that wasn't too good, but that only came from people that wanted to keep her down. Once she called on God and gave her life to Him, it no longer mattered what people thought; as long as she had Him, her family, and her best friends, she was good.

"Ahhhhhhhhhhhhh! Good morning boo!" Dominique greeted her receptionist Kina in her normal animated fashion.

No matter what time or how busy the shop was, Dominique made sure to make the atmosphere a lively one. She didn't do drama too much, but she sure didn't mind sipping a lot of the tea that was poured on the daily, when she was open. Some of the things that the ladies would talk about would have her crying and in tears so much, she would have to take a break just to get herself together.

"Morning boss lady, you look cute today," Kina said. Dominique was rocking a simple pair of jeans with a cream colored sweater and some brown flats. It was a little breezy outside but not enough to where she needed her winter coat. For March it was pleasant, but that could all change in a matter of minutes.

Dominque had recently gotten her hair cut in a short pixie cut that fit her face perfectly.

"Thank you love. How many heads do I have today?" she asked to make sure she had all of her ducks in a row. If there was one thing that she hated was to be unorganized when it came to her business.

"Umm, you have one at ten, twelve thirty, three, four, and six," Kina said looking at her schedule. Dominique loved how Kina was always on her job and it made it easy for not just Dominique to run smoothly, but the other stylists as well.

"What is my twelve thirty getting?"

"That's Mother Joyce so she's getting the usual wash and set," Kina replied.

Mother Joyce had been coming to her since she opened her salon and she was one of the wisest old ladies she had ever met. Since she had never gotten the chance to meet her either of her grandmothers, Mother Joyce filled that void. She first met her when she started going to Blessed Calvary and since then, she has been something like a mentor for her. Whenever she needed understanding about anything, from a relationship with God to a relationship with men, she was there giving the best advice that she could, and Dominique appreciated her for that.

"Okay, that won't take long. Can you put me down for lunch at two, please?"

"It's already done. When I saw the time between those two clients and what they were getting done, I went ahead and put you down for lunch," Kina smiled.

"See, this is why you earn the salary that you do because you go above and beyond for us and I appreciate it," Dominique said honestly.

"Well, you may think differently when your first appointment gets here," Kina told her trying her best not to laugh.

"Oh Lord. Don't tell me it's Sa—" she began only to be cut off.

"The divaaaaaa has arrived! Come through hunty, yasss!" Samson said coming in twirling. One of those days he was gonna twirl so hard and that foot was going to slip from under him and land him right on his behind.

Dominique didn't have anything against Samson, but he was so extra all the time. He reminded her of that blogger Funky Dineva, with his scrawny body and extravagant clothing. He always wanted to do something outlandish with his hair and no matter how many times Dominique would disagree with the style, in the end, it was him that had to wear it.

All eyes were on Samson as he strutted back and forth in front of the receptionist desk, like he was modeling in New York Fashion Week. Only this was the collection nobody wanted to see. He was wearing one of those beauty supply store scarves that had 'Jesus' written all over it with the gold crosses. Dominique knew where he got it from because she had the same red and gold one.

He had the shades that came from the front counter of the same store and wrapped around his body was a full-length polyester coat that had some fake fur around the neck. Samson tried to tell them it was chinchilla and they let him have it. If that was the lie that he wanted to be sent to hell for telling, that was strictly on him. There was no way that squirrel hair around his neck was chinchilla, but if he liked it they loved it.

The best part of the outfit though, was when he took that coat off. Dominique was so glad that she didn't have to go to the bathroom because if she did, she was sure she would have been standing in a pool of her own pee by now.

Samson was on the short side for a man, although he didn't consider himself one, and he had to weigh ninety-three pounds soaking wet, with rocks in his pockets, at the most. When he opened that coat and reveled his purple cat suit with the rhinestones, the salon erupted in laughter.

The look on his face was priceless but he was not moved.

"Oh, I see y'all jealous wombats hating early in the morning. Come on queen, come fix my hair so that I can shut them down completely!" he said, snapping his fingers and grabbing Dominique's hand, leading her towards her station. Today was about to be one for the books.

***

Dominique walked over to the dryer to check and make sure that Samson's hair was dry. This fool wanted gold finger waves on the left side of his hair, with purple pin curls in the front; a high bun that had green baby doll curls coming from the top and beads hanging from the ends.

There was no way on the face of the earth that Dominique could make this hairstyle look cute, but she wasn't the one that had to wear it. Once he was done, he headed straight to the mirror and 'bout lost his mind.

"Queen, this is fierce hunty! I'm 'bout to shut them down at Mardi Gras next week on Fat Tuesday!" he said excitedly.

Once again, everyone within ear shot doubled over in laughter. This time Dominque had tears in her eyes and had to sit in her own chair just to catch her breath.

"Wait Samson! You do know that Mardi Gras was last month in February right?" one of the stylists Sylvia asked, as she wiped her tears from her face.

With that ensemble, hair, and makeup Samson was sporting, he did look like he needed to be on somebody's parade float but he had missed that one for the year.

WHY WON'T HE LOVE ME?

Samson was so distraught about missing the holiday that he didn't even care how weak people were around him. Usually, he would give a few people a nice little read, but today he just couldn't do it. He paid Dominique for her services, flamboyantly placed his shades on his face and coat around his shoulders, and sashayed out the door.

Dominque had just gotten herself together when the last person she wanted to see walked through the salon doors.

Lord, keep me near the cross and have my ram in the bush, 'cause if this broad says one thing out of line, I'm flipping over tables like Jesus did that one time, Dominque said silently as she stared into the face of her baby daddy's wife.

-4-

When Michael woke up that morning and decided that he wanted to spend the day with Kajuana, it was kind of bittersweet for her. She was glad that it would be just them but then on the other hand, she felt like he was only doing it out of guilt.

For the last few months, she had seen the signs of something being wrong but had yet to say anything to him. Her intuition was on high alert but she didn't have anything concrete to bring to him, so until then she would just keep her eyes open.

Kajuana got excited when she saw they had arrived at Laser Quest. She loved doing fun things with Michael, and coming to the place where they had their first date warmed her heart.

"I know that I've been a little distant lately and I'm sorry. I just wanted to make it up to you," he said looking at her as he shut the car off. Just looking at her husband made her feel like she was the luckiest woman in the world because he chose her.

Michael was around five-feet-ten with caramel colored skin. He kept a bald head and had a long thick beard that he made sure to keep trimmed neatly. His build was that of a football player because of him constantly being in the gym. Kajuana knew she had a good man but now, things were just different.

Instead of dwelling on the issue right then, she leaned over as she kissed him on his lips and told him to come on so they could head inside.

They had only been in the arcade for about an hour and a half and this was Michael's third time walking off to answer his phone. Kajuana wanted so badly to call him on it, but something just wouldn't let her.

It was twenty minutes later and Michael still hadn't returned, so she got up to head to the front. Walking back to the entrance, she didn't see him and thought that maybe he was just in the bathroom. Kajuana didn't mind walking up in the men's restroom, but she didn't want to embarrass anyone, so she asked one of the men at the payment counter to go and see if he was in there. She gave him her husband's name and waited for him to return, only to tell her that no one was in there.

Thanking him, she walked towards the exit to see if maybe he was out there or possibly had been in the car. To Kajuana's surprise, Michael was nowhere to be found and neither was their car!

"Now I know darn well..." she trailed off as she pulled her phone out of her purse and proceeded to call him.

She had to have called over twelve times, only for her call to be sent straight to the voicemail. Not bothering to leave a message or text him, she placed a call to Santana. Hopefully she was free and could come right away. No matter how hard she tried, she could not understand how in the world her husband would just up and leave her like that.

"Hey bookie!" Santana answered.

"Can you come get me sis?" Kajuana huffed. She had hoped her friend would just agree and not ask her any questions right now. If she did, she wouldn't be able to force the cry that she felt coming up, back down.

"Where are you, I'm on my way?" Thank God for friends that knew something was wrong and knew when to ask questions and when it wasn't the right time.

"Laser Quest."

"Okay, give me a few minutes and I'm on the way."

"Thanks sis," Kajuana said before hanging up.

Normally it took about thirty minutes to get to where she was from Santana's house, but she made it in just under twenty.

The whole time she waited, she continued to call Michael's phone only to get the same results. She didn't mean to slam Santana's car door when she got in, but she couldn't help it. Her attitude was on ten and she didn't know what to do. Before she could fill Santana in, she got a notification on her banking app that said there had been a sizeable withdrawal from an account that she hadn't touched.

When she started seeing the changes in Michael and their joint account was depleting at a rapid pace, she knew she had to do something. So she opened a new one so that they would still have money for their needs. She was not about to be left with nothing and homeless.

Her breath was almost taken from her body, as she held her chest looking at the negative balance. Tears threatened to fall and her head was spinning. How could this be possible?

"Sis, you okay, what's wrong?" Santana asked with a worried look on her face. As soon as she heard Kajuana take in a deep breath, she knew something was seriously wrong. She was about to just let it ride for a minute until Kay was ready to talk, but this made her nervous.

She was already wondering what she was doing out here without her car. The last thing Santana knew was that today, Kajuana and Michael were spending the day together. Waiting for a response to her question was torture because she wanted to know what was going on.

"No, no, no!" Kajuana said while she frantically searched through her wallet looking for something.

Whatever she was looking for must not have been there because when she gave up the search, she laid her head back on the seat and cried.

"He took it all," was all she said.

"Who took what?" Santana asked.

"Michael cleaned out the whole account that I set up once I started noticing he was taking from our joint account. It's negative."

"How in the world did he get to it if he didn't know about it?" Santana inquired.

Going through her transactions, she saw three for Renaissance Chicago O'Hare Suites Hotel and her heart dropped. What made it worse was the fact that he had just paid for a room ten minutes ago.

Had this man really left her stranded to go be with another woman and with the money she had saved up for them? Kajuana's heart felt like it was being stepped on and she didn't know what to do.

Reaching over and snatching the phone out of her hand, Santana looked at the information on the screen. Without another word, she hit a quick left and headed in the direction of the hotel. Anger was taking over her because she just couldn't understand how Michael could be doing this to his wife.

Kajuana was so distraught that she didn't even realize where they were going because she was crying so hard. She had only made it a few blocks before her phone started ringing. She knew it was Dominique by her ringtone. The last thing that she needed right now was for Dominique to know about Michael and Kajuana's situation. She would make the situation worse, so Santana decided to ignore the call until later. Right now, she needed to go and find out what her best friend's husband was up to.

When Santana pulled into the parking lot of the hotel, was the first time that Kajuana noticed where they were.

"No Tana! I can't do this right now. Just take me home and let me figure out what's going on," Kajuana pleaded. She knew that she needed answers but she didn't think that she was really ready to face the truth.

She wasn't sure how she would respond if the man that she loved more than anything in the world was there with another woman.

Looking over at her friend, Santana saw the pain as well as the fear that was displayed in her eyes, and she softened a bit. She hadn't stopped to even consider how her girl was feeling after just finding out her husband was robbing them blind and possibly all for another woman.

"I'm sorry sis, I was reacting on my feelings instead of thinking about yours," Santana told her just as she was about to put the car in drive to leave and return Dominique's call.

"This no good dirty dog!" Kajuana yelled with her eyes getting big as she snatched her seatbelt off and opened her door.

Santana turned in the direction Kajuana was walking, and saw Michael coming out of the lobby of the hotel. She knew this was about to be all bad if she didn't intervene and fast.

Not even bothering to turn the car off, Santana hopped out right behind Kajuana. Michael had a look of dread on his face as he looked down at his phone. He was so into what he was doing that he didn't even notice his wife coming until it was too late.

"So this what we doing now Michael?" she asked right before hitting him in the back of his head. She was raining blow after blow and Santana could tell that he didn't even have the energy to try and stop her. He knew that he was caught and he knew that whatever he had been doing was the cause of his wife reacting like she was. The last thing that he wanted to do was hurt the woman that he loved, and if she would just give him a few moments and calm down, he would explain everything to her.

"Come on Kay, don't do this baby, let me explain," Michael pleaded, doing the best he could in order to protect his face.

"Explain what Michael? How you spending all of our money on weed and women? The money we worked so hard for!" Kajuana yelled while trying to catch her breath. She was swinging so hard and fast that it was causing her to get light headed.

"You mean the money that you tried hiding from me? I found the other account information and bank card Kay!" Michael yelled back like he had a leg to stand on and by the look on Kajuana's face, she was about to kick that one right from under him too.

"You doggone right! How else was I supposed to make sure that we were protected since you thought I was oblivious to the fact that you were taking money out of our joint account? How was I supposed to feel knowing that we may not be able to make our mortgage or car payments because my husband was putting our money elsewhere? And on top of all of that, you are spending it on another woman Michael!" she screamed, once again going after his head and face.

Santana tried her best to break them apart. She knew that Michael would never hit Kajuana, but she was landing some blows that were so hard and heavy she couldn't be mad at him if his reflexes kicked in.

"You're right! You're right! I'm sorry Kay," he said defeated, finally able to remove himself from her grip with a little assistance from Santana.

"But baby, I promise that I'm not cheating on you with another woman," he tried defending himself. Michael may have gotten his point across, had one of the prettiest females she had ever seen not walk out at that very moment.

The look on his face was priceless. It looked like he was trying to keep his face neutral and emotionless, but he had never been one that could hide how he was feeling. That's one of the ways Kajuana knew that something was off lately, because Michael's normal happy demeanor was gone and had been replaced with a stressful one.

Both Santana and Kajuana's attention went to the woman as she walked in their direction. She wasn't even paying attention to them as she had her head down, searching through her Mouawad 1001 Nights Diamond purse. Had this been any other time, Santana would have stopped her to talk about that masterpiece.

When they first came out back in 2011, she was in awe and even though she could afford the hefty price tag, she couldn't see herself spending money like that on a bag that would require her to have armed guards surrounding her if she was out in public.

Not only was this woman's purse a masterpiece, but so was she. Santana couldn't tell what nationality she was, but she knew she was not American. She had one of the sickest bodies ever and her face was flawless. She was so put together that Beyoncé would need to step her game up a few notches. Her hair was long and silky, and her skin was the same color as the inside of an almond. Santana was so stuck in her own thoughts that she almost missed what the woman said.

"Same time next week Michael, and this time don't be late," the woman said smiling politely. She obviously didn't know who Kajuana was because the smile she gave her was actually genuine. That was until Kajuana lunged towards her.

It was like a light went off in her head when the realization hit her. Santana prayed this woman didn't say anything, but that prayer went unanswered real quick. It took everything in both Michael and Santana to hold Kay back once she opened her mouth.

"Ohhhh, this must be the wife," she began. "I see why your double life needs to be well hidden. She's pretty and feisty. Maybe I should have had her on my team instead," she smirked at him and turned to wink at Kajuana before walking off.

It was something about that comment that immediately caused Kajuana to stop the fighting she had been doing, long enough to get both Michael and Santana's hands off of her. Without another word or any fight left in her, she headed off towards Santana's car and got in.

"Sis, please—" Michael started only to be cut off by Santana's hand in his face.

"Fix it!" was all she said before walking away.

Once she got in the car, they both just sat there in their own thoughts. Santana wondering why Michael would do something like this, and Kay wondering why God was punishing her. Was it something that she had done in her past and this was what she was reaping from that decision long ago? If so what was it, so that she could repent and ask God to take this pain away?

"Why won't he love me sis?" Kajuana asked sadly. There were no more tears because she had seemingly cried her last ones as she wrapped her arms around herself.

Feeling like she was defeated, Santana sighed before she said, "Sis, I know he loves you. Don't ever doubt that. I just, I just don't know what happened."

"Another woman though, Tana? Why couldn't he just tell me what I was doing wrong so I could have fixed me!" Kajuana yelled. She had gone from feeling sad and disappointed to flat out angry.

Santana understood where her friend was coming from because although she had never been married, she had been in a long committed relationship where she was engaged.

Donovan had been her college sweetheart and they had made plans to get married after being together for almost five years together. Everyone including Santana thought they were the perfect couple, until she came home unexpectedly from a literary conference and caught him in their bed with another woman.

He gave her some lame excuse about her career, making her feel like she was superior to him because she made more money than he did. Never once did she intentionally throw around money in their relationship. If anything, she only tried to help him get the business he wanted to start off the ground, but he would never take her money. She tried to be supportive of everything he did, but somewhere there was a disconnect. That was the main reason she found it so hard to date because her career and success was always the center of attention and it wasn't good attention. She had made her decision two years ago that the next man she was interested in would get to know her for who she was before they knew what she did. Maybe, just maybe they would accept her.

The question that Kajuana had just asked rang true in Santana's life as well, and she hadn't even realized it until that moment. Would anyone ever love her for her?

"You better answer Nique before she sends out a search party for you," Kajuana said, looking out of the window and bringing Santana from her thoughts.

While reaching for her phone that had stopped ringing, she watched as Michael and Kajuana both watched one another with tears and hurt all over their faces. Now that the heat of the moment was passing and things were cooling off, Santana saw something in Michael's eyes that told her that this may not be what they actually thought it was. Or then again, it could have been what he wanted them to think. She didn't know, but she was sure that soon all would be revealed. The question was would Kay be ready when the truth was finally given to her.

Dominique's ringtone started up again and Santana realized that Nique had called her over ten times making this number eleven.

"Hey boo," Santana answered, trying her best to sound chipper, but that was cut short when she heard her sister screaming on the other end.

"WHERE THE HECK YOU BEEN AND WHY YOU NOT ANSWERING YOUR PHONE? NEVER MIND, SOMEBODY BETTER HAVE SOME BAIL MONEY 'CAUSE I JUST GOT IT POPPIN AND I KNOW THAT SCARY BROAD LIKES TO CALL THEM BOYS IN BLUE! MESS AROUND AND I BE THAT GIRL IN ORANGE!" Dominique yelled. She was so loud that Santana had to move the phone away from her ear.

Even with Kajauna going through her situation, hearing her friend going off immediately caught her attention, as she looked over at Santana. That was one thing that the three of them often did. No matter what they were going through personally and how bad it was, they made sure to still be there for one another.

"Nique, where are you?" Santana asked, finally putting her car in gear and pulling off. Now that the Michael situation had gotten somewhat under control, here she was going to referee something else. The last thing she wanted was for Dominique to go to jail.

"At work and this ole no neck bum think I care about tearing this place up. Babyyyy, she just don't know, my account is stacked and I can get everything replaced!"

Santana made a right at the light so that she could now head in the direction of Dominque's shop. Santana had removed the phone from her hand and placed it on speaker so she could continue to drive and hear at the same time.

"Nique, what's going on sis?" Kajuana knew who Dominique was referring to when she said 'no neck'. The only person she called that was her baby daddy, Kendrae's wife. They were forever going at it when Dominique didn't even want him. She had made it clear so long ago, but for some reason he still wasn't trying to hear it and neither was Qwayla.

Qwayla was the type that was insecure about a man that she knew she was sharing with every female around the way. It bothered her that even though Dominique's past was attached to a bad reputation, she was still about her business and she was trying to get herself together for not just her kids, but herself.

It was like once Dominique had their son, Kendrae got sloppy with his cheating. Of course, Dominique had her suspicions about him, but she never did have any proof. She may have only been sixteen at the time, but she was smart. Neither was she one of those females that would always nag her man because of what she thought. Without having any concrete evidence, all she could do was sit back and wait, but once she had all that she needed, she would cut them off and not go back.

The day that she saw Kendrae and Qwayla coming out of the courthouse, both sporting wedding bands, it was over for her. Dominique was heading inside to get a copy of her baby's birth certificate, when she saw them heading in her direction. Qwayla thought she had the upper hand considering she was older, pregnant, and now had his last name. She was waiting for a reaction or for Dominique to say something so she could embarrass her, but all she got was a kind smile and a knowing look.

Kajuana would never forget that day. Qwayla let it be known that once she had her baby, she would come see Dominique. Nique told her she would be waiting and that she would tag her face every time she thought she wanted it. She let it be clear that they weren't fighting over a no good man but if she came in her face with disrespect, she would act accordingly.

Over the last few years' things had kind of calmed down, especially with Dominique being in church now, so Kajuana nor Santana couldn't understand what had changed to make Qwayla show up at her shop out of the blue. If they found out that Dominique was messing with Kendrae again, they would be reading her like they did the New Testament.

"I bet you won't! You might jump over here but you gone crawl back!" they heard Dominique say right before she dropped the phone.

Kajuana and Santana had just pulled up in front, and the car was still rolling as they tried to get out. The scene was just like the one from the movie Friday, when Smokey tried to park his car and it kept rolling. Once Santana had the car under control, they both rushed inside to see if they could get Dominique to follow suit.

-5-

It was Sunday morning and Santana had been up for a few hours. Between her eventful day before with Kajuana and Dominique, along with her nerves, she just couldn't rest. Her nerves had her all anxious because she didn't know how she would react and feel if Cortez showed up, or if he decided to skip out on her. She kept thinking that he was only telling her what she wanted to hear at that moment, and just like the other men that had come and gone, he wouldn't keep his promise either.

When she thought about it though, could she really get mad because they really didn't get to talk long so neither of them knew each other. How could she feel any type of way about a stranger?

Staring at herself in her floor-to-ceiling mirror, she was pleased with her look. Today she was rocking her natural in an abundance of curls. Last night she had washed, conditioned, and twisted it up so that she could get the desired look that she wanted. When she added the gold headband and gave her face a slight beat, she was ready to get dressed.

Santana decided on keeping it simple, so she chose a canary yellow blouse, and some navy blue slacks that she realized would be the last go round with. The way they hugged her hips, she knew that if she shouted wrong this here Sunday, something was going to snap but this was what she had decided on wearing the previous night and didn't have time to search for anything else.

Slipping her freshly pedicured feet into her yellow pumps, Santana threw on her blazer to complete her look. Once she was pleased, she emptied her purse before grabbing her clutch and only placing her phone, ID, and bank cards inside.

Walking down the hall, she stopped at her guest room and knocked on the door.

"You almost ready, sis?" Santana asked through the door.

After she and Kajuana had gotten the situation under control at Dominique's shop, the two of them headed back to her house. Kajuana said that she didn't trust herself being around Michael when he got home, so she asked if she could stay the night. Considering it was only Santana living in that big house, she welcomed the company.

Kajuana opened the door fully dressed but with puffy eyes. It was evident to Santana that Kay had spent all night crying because a couple of times she had to go and check on her. Hopefully, church would be what she needed once they got there because they could all use an on time word.

Santana smiled and wiped the corner of Kajuana's eyes and took her by the hand. Locking up the house, they got in the car and were on their way.

The regular service didn't start until ten, but they always made sure to get there no later than nine for their Sunday enrichment groups, or Sunday school as most people called it. This week they were talking about Jacob and Rachael that came out of the book of Genesis.

Everyone was still waiting for Mother Joyce to come in being that she was the leader of their group. When Santana and Kajuana walked inside, it didn't take them long to find Dominique. She had already dropped the kids off for their lessons, and was sitting in their section having a conversation with one of the members.

Just by looking at Dominique and her body language, the ladies could already tell she was still upset from the day before and didn't want to be bothered. Glancing up the moment she felt their presence, her eyes landed right on Kajuana and the sad face she had, and it instantly changed how she was feeling. Dominique's situation didn't even compare to what Kajuana had going on with her husband, so it was easy to put her sister's needs before her own.

Neither Kajuana nor Santana had a chance to say anything before Mother Joyce came in to get started.

"Good morning everyone. Before we get started, I want to introduce my nephew Najir. He just moved here from North Carolina and I am so happy to have him," she said pointing behind where it was the ladies were sitting.

As soon as Dominique turned around and her eyes landed on him, she could have sworn this man had a halo above his head and a bright light illuminating from his body. The man was gorgeous. He looked to be around their age and was the most handsome man she had ever seen.

She didn't know how tall he actually was, but even as he was seated, he still had some height to him. There was one thing that Dominique loved about a man and that was him being tall.

His skin was a pretty smooth chocolate color, almost like Nutella, and his eyes were a deep dark brown. Even when he wasn't smiling, his eyes seemed to and in that moment, she was head over heels. If someone had told her that love at first sight didn't exist, at that very moment she would have called them a demon and cast them back to hell, because she was definitely a believer.

"I'm glad to be here as well Auntie. It's nice to be in the house of the Lord once again," he smiled, and if Santana hadn't been seated right beside Dominique, she never would have believed that her friend had literally swooned when that man opened his mouth to speak.

"My God that sits on the throne," Dominique said under her breath.

Both Santana and Kajuana couldn't help but to stifle their giggles, as they elbowed Dominique so she could stop playing so much. Even Mother Joyce noticed, but all she did was wink her eye at Dominique and did her best to hold back her laughter of her own.

"Well now. Who had a chance to read the lesson this past week?" she asked getting started.

Once everyone gathered their books, they turned to the lesson that came out of the twenty ninth chapter of Genesis. They went over how Jacob fell in love with Rachel and went to her father, Laban and asked for her. It was rare that boys and men these days took that approach, and out of respect went to the father first. They felt like they were grown men and could do what it was they wanted to do, instead of realizing it was the proper thing to do. Then, too, there weren't too many fathers in the home in their rightful places as it was. You can't do something you were never taught, especially if her father is absent too.

"How many of you ladies have ever had a man go to the extremity of sacrificing whatever he had to just to make you his, and how many men have ever, or will ever go through those extremities for a woman that you have no doubt God is presenting you?" Mother Joyce asked.

She was so surprised to see only one hand go up from an unfamiliar face, but she was eager to hear what he had to say, so she gave him the floor.

"Go ahead, sir," she told him.

"This is my first time here, but I know of the story from the lesson and I would have to say that I have never gone to the extreme for a woman, because God had never presented her to me until recently," he said, causing Santana to almost snap her neck as she turned around.

Even if she wanted to, she couldn't help the butterflies she had in her stomach from fluttering, her heart feeling like it was about to jump out of her chest, or the big smile she now had on her face. Dominique and Kajuana hadn't even been told about her meeting Cortez because of the things going on in their own lives, but here he was sitting on the last row and looking directly into her face.

"I understand what Jacob was feeling when he saw Rachel, and he just knew that no matter what he was going to have her, and whatever he had to do to get her he would do, even if it made him uncomfortable," Cortez continued.

"Oh that's good. He was surely uncomfortable, especially when his arrangement with her father was violated," Mother Joyce said.

It was true that once the agreement had been made after the time was served by Jacob, Laban still gave him his other daughter Leah instead of Rachel as he had agreed. So many times we make arrangements in not only our personal lives, but business as well and people will bail on us. But if you are steadfast on knowing the promises God has given you, then no matter what, you will endure what you have to in order to get the end result, and that's exactly what Jacob did. In the end, he got the woman that he had worked hard for and sacrificed his own comfort to have.

"I wish a man would do that for me," Dominique said.

"Maybe if you weren't run through so much and at least knew who your kids' fathers were, one would," Brother Andre said. He probably thought he had said it low but everyone heard him, including Dominique. That attitude that she does her best to put away while in church, came to life so fast that there was no doubt his head was swimming.

"Oh, soooo you still mad 'cause I wouldn't let you hit, huh? Let's get this straight or what not," Dominique started. It would have been funny watching her neck roll normally, but considering they were in the Lord's house, it was inappropriate.

"Nah Tana! He thinks he can say what he wants when he wants and won't get checked." Dominique fumed when Santana touched her gently, trying to calm her down before she did something that she would regret later.

"I understand sis, but this is not the place," Kajuana said stepping in.

"Man, bro, that was uncalled for. You don't say stuff like that to a woman, and you definitely don't disrespect God's house by doing it here. Who raised you?" Najir said taking up for Dominique.

Well at least that was what she felt like he was doing. Najir may have been standing up for her, but he was mostly doing it because he hated when a man let their egos, bruised or not, cause them to come at any woman sideways.

"You obviously don't know her," Andre scoffed trying to save face. The looks that everyone was giving him didn't even sway him to realizing that a meeting with their Pastor would soon be on the horizon.

"It don't matter if I know her or not. What kind of godly man would I be to let you disrespect any lady while in my presence? I guess placing that collar around your neck when you became a minister was just a show for you. Let me give you a little insight real quick. A title won't get you into heaven just like some of your body parts won't make you a man," Najir said, turning his attention back to the front.

It was in that moment Dominique had been won over by a man, for the first time in her life. Najir reminded her so much of her uncle and how he lived his life, and since that was the only father figure she had, he was the example of the type of man that she sought after. He held God to the highest regard and his family came before anyone else.

Giving Andre the death stare before turning around, Dominique let her eyes fall on Najir and thanked him. Without a word, he simply nodded his head in her direction and waited for the lesson to resume.

It took a few minutes before they were all settled again and were able to return to the lesson. It bothered Dominique that people couldn't see past who she used to be and understand that she was trying her best to change. She knew there were still some things she had to work on, like her temper and how ratchet she could be, but she was a work in progress.

Once church was over, the three ladies headed out to the front. Santana had been so distracted that she had totally forgotten that Cortez was in attendance and they were supposed to go to lunch together. She stole a few glances at him throughout Sunday school but when Michael walked in for the morning service and Kajuana's emotions took over, she once again let her concern for her friend take precedence.

Today was going to be the official date between her and Cortez and it had totally slipped her mind, until he gently touched her elbow from behind. As soon as she felt that touch, she knew exactly who it was before she even turned around. Santana felt that same connection the day he helped her with her car.

"Hey, you standing me up already beautiful?" he asked with that gorgeous smile that made her blush.

No matter what Dominique and Kajuana were going through in their lives, this made them smile. Giving each other a quick glance, they turned their attention back to their sister, in admiration of the way the man in front of her made it seem like they were the only two in the room. They didn't know him but they liked him already.

Santana was blushing so hard that everyone close to her would have been able to see if she had any cavities at all, from the way she was smiling. They watched as the guy that spoke a few times during class earlier, moved his hand from her elbow down to hold her hand loosely in his. It was so cute that it was sickening.

"Ummmm, this you boo?" Dominique said causing Santana to remember where she was and that she hadn't told them who he was.

"Hopefully," Cortez answered for her.

"Okayyyy, do it big then Papi!" She was so dramatic but they couldn't help but laugh at her.

"Cortez, these are my sisters Kajuana and Dominique," Santana said introducing the three of them.

"It's nice to meet you ladies. So are we still on for our date?" he asked, returning his eyes back to her.

"Date?" both Kay and Nique said with their eyes big and mouths wide open.

Santana wanted to say yes so bad and go, but she didn't want to leave Kajuana considering they rode together and she was staying at her house. Kajuana felt her apprehension and knew that it was because of her, so she stepped in. It had been so long since Santana had found a good guy and was able to go out on a date, so she wasn't going to let her miss this opportunity.

"It was nice meeting you Cortez. Call us later sis. Love you!" Kajuana said, pulling Dominique along with her out of the door before she could object.

"Bih—" Dominique started only to be immediately cut off by Kajuana.

"No ma'am! Don't you dare say that on this good holy ground! You know better," she said chastising her like she was a child.

"You right. You know I be forgetting sometimes or whet not," Dominique said sucking her teeth as they headed towards the building where the youth were during service.

"Why do you do that?" Kajuana asked a confused Dominique.

"Do what?" she asked as they walked.

"Hide behind the ratchet. I mean I still love you ratchet and all, but I just wonder if you did it to mask something else. Like you don't like being vulnerable."

Dominique shrugged instead of answering her because she knew exactly what she meant, and right now she didn't want to talk about why she really was the way that she was. Everything in her life had been an open book to her friends and they thought that they knew everything about her, and they almost did. It was just that one chapter in her book that she had never let anyone read, and she didn't know if she ever would.

By the way Dominique had just responded, Kajuana knew that it was something deep that she didn't want to talk about and instead of pressing her, she would just let it go. In due time it would be revealed, and she would be right there for her sister when it did.

***

It was a blessing to have the children in their own building learning about God, while the adults were able to get fed like they needed to. The distractions were nonexistent for the members, as well as the Pastor. Dominique was always so excited to hear what they had learned about and knowing her oldest, KJ was now one of the youth helpers made her really proud.

"Hey Ms. Allen, how are you?" Kristen asked once Dominque walked into the classroom for the six year olds. They had a different class for each age group so that they could learn on each of their individual levels. The idea was a good one because there was no way that the younger kids could grasp what the teens could, and that made a big difference.

Just like with adults. Some saints are more seasoned in the word because they have been taught or in ministry longer than the ones that may have just come to Christ. The easiest way to drive a new Christian from church was to try and teach them something on a level they knew nothing about. Like teaching Trigonometry to someone who doesn't even know how to add. That would almost like wasting a good word.

"Hey boo! How was my little mama?" Dominique asked her as her daughter ran to her to show her a picture she had drawn.

Not only was she her only daughter, but Quatrice was also her little miracle baby. Tricey, as they affectionately called her, had been born with Sickle Cell Anemia and was in pain most of the time. No matter how much pain she was in, she never felt sorry for herself and she always pushed through with an optimistic attitude. To be so young she had the heart of a warrior, and Dominique was blessed to have her.

When she had first found out about her daughter's condition, Dominique was a mess. First she blamed God, then herself, and even the father. Whoever he was. But when she started to watch her daughter grow and saw how she rolled with the punches, she finally let all of that hatred go for everyone. Tricey didn't even know the impact that she had on her mother and that was the main reason she tried her best to change for all of her kids.

Tricey was a pretty little thing. She had long, thick sandy brown hair that came down her back and it fell beautifully against her light skin. Her eyes were so big and round and stood out because they were two different colors. The left eye was a pretty emerald green color while the other was as blue as the ocean. If Dominique was confused about who her father was before she had Tricey, she was positive she didn't know the minute her daughter opened her eyes for the first time.

"She was so good. Once I taught them about how God created everything, she was just so amazed. She wanted to know more and retained everything that we had talked about. Tricey is a little sponge," Kristen said.

That she could agree with. Sometimes it could be a blessing and a curse, because some things Dominique didn't want her remembering and she picked the most inopportune times to bring them up.

"Bye Mrs. Kristen! See you Sunday," Tricey said heading for the door. That was her way of indicating that she was ready to go.

Laughing at her child, Dominque said her goodbyes as they walked out. As soon as Tricey saw Kajuana standing with her brothers, she high tailed it right to her. Tricey loved her Godmothers and they loved her right back.

"Auntie Mama, are you going to have my little cousin soon?" Tricey asked Kajuana, standing there with her arms wrapped around her waist. She had been asking this question a lot lately, and Dominque could tell this was a sore subject for her. Especially with how things were between her and Michael.

"Not yet baby girl," she told her with a sad smile.

"One day?"

WHY WON'T HE LOVE ME?

"One day, mama."

"Yes! I hope it's going to be a girl so she can have sleepovers with me," Tricey said walking ahead of them. This little girl was a mess but they all loved her nonetheless. Every time Tricey saw either Santana or Kajuana, she would ask the same thing. She wanted a little cousin so bad that she could play with, and made sure to let it be known she preferred a girl.

Dominique's sons were in a world of their own, talking about some video game, when she heard that dreaded voice once again.

"You find out who your baby's daddies were yet? You know they got a show that will pay for the test for you if you can't afford it." It was Brother Andre.

Kajuana knew they were no longer inside of church and she was worried that Dominique would go off in a way that would make even the devil himself embarrassed.

"Let's just go to the car, sis. Ignore him, we have the kids with us," Kajuana said trying to help avoid this train wreck that was about to happen.

"Oh, trust and believe that if I needed something paid for, I could do it on my own," Dominique spoke turning around to face him.

"I bet. Hoeing must pay real good these days," he said smirking, causing Dominique to ball her hands up into tight fists.

"Now that's enough Andre. For one, you are still on the Lord's grounds and two, you are being real disrespectful to my sister in front of her kids." It was now Kajuana's turn to be mad.

She hated when men who had gotten bruised egos, started trying to disrespect a female because she turned them down. That's all that Andre was mad about. Yea, Dominque had a reputation when she was younger, but she was doing all that she could now to turn it around. Everyone wouldn't be happy with her change and she knew that, so when they came at her she was always on the defense.

It was like people hated seeing others better themselves and they weren't even aware that they were being used by the enemy to do his dirty work. Even right there in the church. People were constantly gossiping and backbiting just to keep the next man down, and all because they were mad that someone decided to make a change that they weren't brave enough to do.

Dominique had been through a lot. Most of it was self-inflicted and even then, she never blamed anyone else for her mess ups, but she wasn't about to keep letting people put their negative mouths on her or her children.

"Nah, that's okay sis. I got this or what not." Here comes the ratchet. *Cardi B would be proud,* Kajuana thought, shaking her head.

"I wouldn't know how much hoeing pays. That's something you would have to ask your mother to enlighten you on. As for my kids, keep them out of it. Yeah I like to party and yeah, I done been around the block a few times, but you better believe when I let someone have this, he's always satisfied," Dominique assured him by using her hand to tap on her private area. Kajuana was so glad that her back was turned so the kids didn't see that gesture. It was bad enough they were witnessing everything else that was going on.

Andre's feelings must have been real hurt because what he said next was the ultimate low blow.

"You mean satisfied like ole boy you put that rape charge on? You must have felt like your number was too high when you got with that one, so you hollered rape so it wouldn't count," he smirked.

Rape was nothing that Dominique took lightly. It had taken her months to get out of that depression, and no one knew exactly how she was feeling during that time. Everything she did reminded her of that night, and it took a miracle to bring her out of that state. She understood how other women who had gone through the same thing felt, and it was not a joking matter.

Before Kajuana could react, Dominique had swiftly moved towards him and slapped him as hard as she could. Tricey broke out crying and KJ and Julian were just about to rush over and protect their mother, when she turned around and grabbed them so that they could go to the car.

The tears that rolled down her cheeks felt like flames they were so hot, and all she wanted to do was leave. She had gotten pushed to a point that she had vowed to never let another human being take her to again, and here she was letting Andre have that control.

"I hope to God you repent for all of this before you take your last breath, because you will be busting hell wide open because of this if you don't. And you call yourself a man. Tuh!" Kajuana said walking off towards Dominique's car.

Right before they were able to get in and adjusted, they noticed everyone standing outside stunned at what they had just witnessed. Kajuana and Dominique both knew that no one was looking at them like Dominique was the one to cause the blow up, but you could tell they were shocked at her response. It was no secret about what she had gone through and most of them sympathized with her. Then there were the ones who were so miserable with their own lives that they used the hurt and pain of others to torment them. If that wasn't a trick of the enemy, then they didn't know what was.

Kajuana was a firm believer that there was nothing more pleasing to Satan than him continuing to hurt people with the mistakes or shortcomings every chance he got. When we didn't let go of things like that and forgive not only others but ourselves, he played on that. And at that moment, he felt like he had another victory over Dominique, but God would soon show him that He would always be undefeated when it came to the wellbeing of His children.

Putting the car in gear, Dominique headed out of the parking lot. Wiping her face, she tried to calm her nerves so that she could drive without getting into an accident. Her eyes were blurry and her hands were shaking like a leaf.

"Wait sis, let me drive. You are in no condition to be behind the wheel."

Refusing to debate with Kajuana, she did as she was told and put the car in park. As she was rounding the front of the car, her eyes locked on Najir momentarily. Something about him was calming and she felt like she had just been given a fresh breath of air, only for it to be taken away again. Najir took her breath away just with his presence, and she wished that she could get to know him better, but after being a witness to her second fall out, she was sure that he had heard all that he needed to hear in order not to have anything to do with her. She was feeling like a man like him would never love a woman like her, so there was no need to go any further.

Najir watched as she turned her head and proceeded to get in on the passenger side. Initially, when he first saw her that morning he was attracted to her, but that was quickly in question when she started arguing with Andre in church and now again after service.

Granted, Andre was out of line, but the things he heard come from the both of them made it hard for him to ever see if there could be anything more. He felt like if a woman couldn't even act classy in church, then she was sure to be a force to be reckoned with outside of it.

Najir got in his own car to wait on his aunt, as he watched Dominique ride away. She was so beautiful to him and the fact that she had kids didn't bother him at all. What bothered him was the fact of how she had gotten them. To hear Andre talking about paternity tests was a red flag for him, so he decided to just wave his own white flag in surrender of getting to know her.

-6-

Santana sat on the passenger side of Cortez's truck as he headed to wherever it was he was taking her for brunch. It was barely noon when church let out, so they had some time to find somewhere good to eat before closing.

Jeremih's voice crooned through the speakers of the truck and it relaxed her so much that she found herself resting her head on the headrest and her arm on the center console. She had closed her eyes, and immediately they popped open again when she felt his arm touch her skin.

"You don't have to move." He smiled when he saw her sit upright again and move her arm away. It wasn't because she didn't want to be near him, but she didn't want him thinking she was trying to be all up in his space.

"I didn't mean to be all up under you like that," she apologized to him.

"What if I don't mind you being up under me? That shows me that you're comfortable around me and that's what I want."

Cortez sounded so sincere when he said that and the look on his face matched what he was saying. What was it about this man that had her feeling like she was falling? And falling fast.

Before she could respond, she saw that they were pulling up to Wildberry Pancakes and Café. This was one of her favorite places and she was excited that he put some thought into where to take her. She had honestly thought he was going to take her to get something quick, or perhaps IHOP. It wouldn't matter one way or the other as long as she was around him. This man seemed to ooze something that was indescribable.

They held all of their conversation until they got inside and once they ordered their drinks, the questions began.

"So are you from here?" Santana asked breaking the ice. For him to have brought her to this specific place he had to have either been a native or did a google search for it.

"I've been here since I was about four, when my family moved from California. When I was in the eleventh grade, my parents got a divorce and my father went back home, while my sister and I decided to stay here with her. I couldn't understand why my father would leave his family, but that's just how it goes, you know?" he disclosed. Santana was glad that he was okay with opening up to her like he was, and she could listen to him all day.

"That must have been tough on you all," she replied.

He took a sip of his drink before he continued.

"Yeah, because he was supposed to be our protector. For a few months after he left, I watched my mother struggle and it broke me. I felt like I had to step up and become the man of the house. I didn't finish school and tried to make a quick hustle that landed me catching a charge."

He was putting it all out there because he wanted to be an open book for her. He felt some type of connection to her, and the last thing he wanted was to move on together and then she find out something that could potentially cause them not to work. Cortez understood the importance of honesty, and that was one thing that he didn't get from his father. His father had lied so long to them all, and once his other family came to the light, he knew then that he would never lie to the woman that he decided to be with. He had seen the devastation that it caused his mother.

"Wow, that's deep. I commend you for stepping up like that. Do you mind telling me how long you were in for?" Santana asked. She had hoped she wouldn't offend him but it was something she was curious about.

"I was just going on nineteen and they gave me six years. I've been out for a little over two years now."

"You're twenty-seven too?"

"Yeah, just had a birthday last month."

Just then their food was brought out to them, and they took a minute for him to say grace before they ate some. Santana had ordered a stack of Banana Cream Pancakes along with a ham and cheese omelet, and Cortez had ordered Cranberry Pecan Pancakes with a Denver skillet that had hash browns, eggs, ham and some more stuff thrown in there.

"So what is it that you do?" he asked her, taking a bite of his pancakes.

They had already talked about her being a military brat and how close she was to Kajuana and Dominique since she was the only child, and she had dreaded the whole career question. She did her best to try and stay as far away as she could from that topic, and she thought she had done a good job of it until now.

It seemed like once she told men about what she did and they found out how much money she made, they were either intimidated and felt like they couldn't compete with her salary and her being her own boss, or they tried to turn her into their sugar mama. She just didn't understand it, and that was one of the reasons she hadn't gone on a date in ages, and put all of her focus in to church and her job.

He must have felt her apprehension so he spoke again.

"You a drug queen pin or something?" he asked trying to lighten the mood.

"Boy no. My scary behind would be so nervous about getting robbed or sent to jail that I would probably tell on myself," she laughed. "I work for a publishing company, nothing glamorous."

Something in her answer told him that she was not being all the way truthful and he didn't want to start off on the wrong foot, so he spoke on it.

"I know that we are just meeting one another and we aren't going to know everything all at once about the other, but I'm big on honesty. I live my life like an open book because I have experienced firsthand how secrets can destroy families, and I want no parts of that. I don't know where this is going and I hope that I can see you again, but I don't want us lying to one another. You feel me?"

Santana understood clearly what he was saying and she wanted so bad to tell him, but couldn't find it in herself right now. She was going to have to see where this thing went with them before she would divulge that piece of information. More than anything, she wanted Cortez to like her for who she was, and not for how many zeros she had in her bank account.

"I totally agree," she said smiling, as they continued to eat their meal and just enjoy each other's company.

-7-

The drive to Dominique's was a quiet one. Neither she nor Kajuana wanted to talk about what had happened in front of the kids. They had seen too much as it was and they didn't want to add to it.

KJ only asked his mother if she was okay once, and as soon as she told him she was, it was as if all was right in the world for them, and she wanted nothing more than to keep it that way. The two of them listened as the kids chatted amongst themselves, leaving the two friends to quietly talk. Since they didn't want to touch Dominique's subject, she decided to fill her sister in on what had gone wrong.

"So I didn't get to tell you this yesterday because of what went down at the shop," she began as she switched lanes. The driver in front of her was driving incredibly slow and she couldn't take it anymore.

Dominque gave her, her undivided attention as she continued to fill her in on everything.

"Remember I told you and sis that Michael wanted to spend the day with me yesterday?" she asked.

"Yeah. 'Bout time he got some act right in his system," Dominique spat.

"Not exactly. If he did, it didn't last long at all."

"Whatchu mean?" she wanted to know, running her words together like she normally did when she was about to get amped up.

"He took me to Laser Quest. You know we like having fun there, so I thought it was cute. Like, he actually put some thought into taking me somewhere that he knew meant something to the both of us."

"Uh huh." By now Dominique was turned with her back facing the door and looking dead into Kajuana's mouth, waiting on the good part.

"Everything was fine until he kept getting these calls and texts. At first he was ignoring them, and then he started walking off to talk on the phone. I was getting irritated by the minute."

"You too soft sometimes, I swear. Did I not teach you anything? You know had that been me, the first call he got and didn't answer I would have been all on top of his head," Dominique said imitating how she would be on top of someone's head.

Kajuana couldn't help but to laugh because she knew it was true. Dominique may have just been on a thousand a little while ago, but somehow she knew how to make light out of a situation to put a smile on her girl's face.

"Anyway fool, the last time he walked off on the phone he was gone a good little bit, so I decided to go and look for him. I even had one of the workers check the men's bathroom and he wasn't there. That was when I walked out to the parking lot and his car was gone."

"You better shut your mouth and sing a song! No that old three nostrils, baldheaded mama having, cross eyed sister having, wanna be a player did not leave my sister! Ohhhh bay bayyyyy, you need to head to my uncle's house so I can drop my babies off and we go to your house. I done already traumatized them once today so I can't do it again."

Kajuana didn't know what she was looking in the mirror for, but she guessed Dominique was just doing stuff to try and calm her nerves.

"That's not all," Santana said knowing this was about to send her over the edge. She hoped that Dominique wouldn't show out too bad, but they weren't too far from her house by then if she needed to tell the kids to go inside so they wouldn't hear their mother.

"Don't tell me nothing else stupid he did. My pressure already high and I don't have any alcohol to calm my nerves. You know I been laid the trees to rest but this here 'bout to make me go call Tony and have him bring me a dub. Better yet, call Michael and tell me to bring me some out of his stash since this is all his fault."

"As soon as I got into the car with Tana, I got a notification on my phone through my bank app. A little while ago when I noticed money being taken from our account, I opened a new one just in case of emergencies."

"You are so smart. I would have never thought about doing that. I would have just been on top of his head again."

"Stop interrupting, dang!" Kajuana couldn't help but to laugh.

"Lord. So the notification came through that all of the money had been withdrawn and was now negative. What made it worse was when I saw that there were a few charges, and one that had been made right after he left me stranded was at a hotel. That's where we were when you kept calling us and didn't get an answer," Kajuana finally got out.

"Guh, what happened when y'all got there and why didn't you call me? I could have fought Qwayla another day chile," Dominique said a little too hype for Kajuana.

"Well, when we were pulling up he was coming out of the hotel, and all I saw was red. I hopped out the car and went in."

"Wheeeeet? No little Miss Demure didn't get to throwing them hands on lil' buddy!" Dominique fell out laughing. Although it wasn't funny yesterday, today Kajuana had to admit it was a little amusing the way Dominique was acting.

"Auntie Mama, you were being ratchet too?" Tricey asked showing all of her little teeth. She must have thought that was the funniest thing ever at the moment.

"Tricey, what I tell you about being in grown folks' business?" Dominique asked as she turned around in her seat. That was one thing that she didn't play when it came to her kids, and that was them jumping in an adult's conversation. It was also another reminder that she needed to be aware of how she acted in front of them.

"So then what happened? Don't tell me he put his hands on you!" Dominique continued.

"Of course not, but I knew that he may have wanted to. I was letting him have it until she came out," Kajuana said glancing over to get Dominique's reaction.

The look on Dominique's face was priceless and right before she could get her sentence formulated, they rounded the corner down from her house and both of their eyes landed on Michael sitting in her driveway.

"KJ, when we get out, I want you to take your sister and brother in the house. Okay?" Dominique instructed to the oblivious child.

"Yes ma'am," KJ told her as they pulled in. She immediately pulled her keys from the ignition once the car was parked, and handed him her house key.

"Bye Auntie Mama," they all said to Kajuana. It was funny how instead of calling her or Santana just 'aunt' or 'God momma' they combined the two.

"See you later Auntie Mama's babies," Kajuana responded and blew them a kiss.

Before KJ could get the front door closed good, Dominique was jumping out of the car and headed straight in Michael's direction. This was not about to be good and Kajuana just prayed for his sake that Dominique didn't act out 'jumping on his head' literally.

-8-

"Girl, naw!" Santana said as she watched Dominique act out how she had jumped on Michael's head. She tried so hard not to laugh, but the visual she was given had her holding her stomach, doubled over in laughter.

Dominique and Kajuana had called to let Santana in on what happened that day after church, but she was either with Cortez or working. Today was the first time that they had been able to actually meet up face to face and catch up.

Although Dominique was trying to make light of the situation, Santana could see from the look in Kajuana's eyes that she was still hurt. The fight between her and Michael had happened well over a week and a half ago, and she was still struggling. And rightfully so. Instead of feeling like she was a burden on either of her friends, Kajuana decided to stay in a hotel so that she could have time to herself.

If she wasn't at the hospital doing her twelve hour shifts then she was laying around in her hotel room sulking. Lately she had been dodging Michael when he would popup at her job as well as his constant calls. Currently she was in her room eating ice cream and listening to Babyface and Toni Braxton's *Love, Marriage, and Divorce* album. She could have sworn that everything they were singing about was her life at the moment, and although she didn't want the divorce coming to pass, she didn't know if that was the direction they were heading in.

When they had pulled up to Dominique's house that day and Michael was in her driveway, it was like Kay had lost her voice and Nique picked it up for her. Michael started off trying to apologize, but that fell on deaf ears. There was nothing that he could say that would make them understand why he had left his wife stranded, took all of their money, and had been in the presence of another woman in a hotel. Kajuana made it clear that everything they had belonged to the both of them, and had he just talked to her about it they could have worked things out.

The theory she had of him smoking again was still there, but his actions were now telling her that something else was going on, and with someone else to say the least. Kajuana didn't even care about the smoking anymore. She had known when she met Michael that he was a smoker, and it didn't bother her too much because every now and again, she would puff one or two with him. But that was before she made the decision to really do her best to live for God. Kajuana still had her shortcomings just like anyone else, so she wouldn't dare judge him for that. All she wanted to do was be there for her husband to find out what was going on, and help him to work on things. In order to do that, she would need him to be honest with her and right now, he couldn't give her that.

"So what did he say to you, sis?" Santana asked.

"He started saying he was sorry and it's not what it looked like. He didn't mean to leave me but he got caught up. Just a whole bunch of nonsense. I could look at him and tell that he was still keeping something from me and until he is ready to be totally honest, there isn't anything I can really do," she said sadly.

"Are you ladies ready to order?" their regular waitress asked, interrupting their conversation.

Once again, they were at their favorite kick back spot, Joe's Crab Shack, and once they left, they would be heading to Santana's house for the rest of their girls' weekend. Dominique's aunt and uncle had her babies for the weekend since they were going to visit family in New York. Dominique would have loved to have gone with them, but she was in serious need of some 'mommy time' so she decided to pass.

Randi, their waitress had impeccable service, and whenever she was working she made sure to be the one to serve them. She was a young girl and they knew that she was still in school, so they made it their business to sow a seed into her life every time they came. They had even invited her to church a few times but with her schedule, she wasn't always able to make it.

"Yes we are. We will have our regular orders Ran," Santana said.

"Well, I won't be having the drink. Can I just get a Sprite mixed with a vanilla Coke and a shot of sweet and sour mix please?" Kajuana ordered. While she flipped through her phone, she didn't even notice the look that all three ladies were giving her.

"What?" she shrugged.

Randi gave her a raised eyebrow and walked off to place their orders, while Dominique and Santana waited for answers. It may not have been unusual if Kajuana was one to drink pop, but for as long as they could remember she never drank it, and would often chastise them for doing so. Especially Dominique. She kept at least three cases of different types of pop on standby on the regular.

"You drinking pop now?" Dominique asked getting her attention.

Looking up from her phone, she shrugged her shoulders like it was normal and returned her eyes back to her screen.

"Y'all, The Shade Room be on point with all of their updates. I wonder how they get all of this information. Celebs must leak it to stay relevant," she said before placing her phone back down and turning her attention to Santana.

"So how are things with you and Cortez?" she sang. Just that fast, Santana's focus was on her new boo and she couldn't help but to blush.

"Oh snap, look at those cheeks turning red and whetnot!" Dominique quipped.

"Do you always have to sound like that girl?" Santana asked. Sometimes it was funny, but then there were times that she just got carried away. It was like she was in character or something, and maybe needed rehab from ratchet TV for a while.

Dominique shrugged her shoulders as she popped her lips, but said nothing else.

"Cortez is everything y'all! He's so attentive when I talk to him. He's spontaneous, loves his family, and most importantly he loves God."

"Don't forget the brother is fine as wine!" Kajuana said drinking from her straw and causing Santana to fall out laughing.

"What's so funny?"

"It's just the first time I saw him, that was my private nickname for him. Even after I found out his name, I was secretly calling him Mr. Fine as Wine."

"You are so corny," Dominique laughed.

"Well, since I'm corny and I guess you stay poppin', what's going on with you and Mother Joyce's nephew?" Santana asked, trying her best to sound like Dominique.

"Girl, not a thing. Crazy thing is I know he's feeling me, but he never gives me the time of day," she said looking a little disappointed.

See, Dominique's problem was that she had never been rejected by a man, she was always the one doing the rejecting. When she set her eyes on someone that she wanted to get to know, she always got it, so this was different for her.

Dominique told them how she had seen him at least four different times this past week, and each time he played her to the left. Even when he dropped his aunt off to get her hair done, he only gave her two words and that was 'hi' and 'bye'. She couldn't figure it out and honestly, she didn't have time to. If he knew her he knew where to find her.

"Are you looking for something for right now or something serious?" Kajuana asked after they decided to just get their food to go. The ladies paid their bill and headed out of the restaurant.

Dominique gave her a smug look instead of responding to the question, so Santana stepped in with her two cents.

"Come on now Nique, who knows you better than we do? We know you have your chosen few that you like to keep around when you need to be broken off, and you never take any of them seriously," she said as she started the car.

"Whatchu trying to say? You calling me loose? The shade is real today!" Dominique said sounding like she was upset. And in a way she was, but not with her friends but herself.

Dominique knew that once she got saved that she wouldn't be changed overnight, but she felt like she had been walking with Christ long enough that she shouldn't still be doing the same things she was doing before she made that commitment. No matter how many times she went to church, laid at the altar, read her bible, or got prayed over, she was still weak in that area.

"Not at all, sis. You know this is a no judgement zone, but we are required to be honest with one another. Don't get me wrong, I see a lot of growth in you, but I also know the area that you are having the biggest struggle in," Santana sincerely stated.

Instead of either of them responding right then, they were each caught up in their own thoughts. Letting them know that she had to make one quick stop before they got to her house, Santana pulled into the Walgreens that wasn't too far from her home. Before she got out, she asked if they needed anything and told them she would be right back.

Although the radio wasn't loud, Dominique could still hear Tink singing her every thought and emotion at the moment. She began to wonder if it was too much to just want somebody to treat her like somebody. Just to forget about her past, see through her flaws, and didn't just want her for one thing. It was now time to be honest with herself and understand that she deserved better. Maybe that's why Najir could never love a woman like her. She knew that he had heard everything that

Andre said about her at church and as much as she had hoped that didn't matter to him, she had to keep it real with herself.

A few minutes had gone by before Santana made her way back to the car, and they headed to her house. Dominique assumed that she had gone to get a few more snacks for the night by the amount of bags she had. They would always have way more snacks that they needed and by Monday morning, they would be regretting their decisions to try and eat it all. They would normally stay in all weekend and not care about anything on the outside of the house.

Neither of the women spoke until they had arrived, but it wasn't one of those uncomfortable silent times. It was welcomed. Once they made it inside, they changed into their pajamas, put their snacks in the stash spots, grabbed a few drinks and headed to the living room. They were just about to pick a movie on demand when Santana stopped Kajuana from sitting down.

"No ma'am. Don't sit down, go take this then come back," she said handing her a plastic Walgreens bag.

Both Dominque and Kajuana had the same confused looks on their faces as they looked at Santana.

"Don't look at me like that heffa. You forget we know each other like the backs of our hands and when something changes, we know there is an underlying reason. Just like Dominique looking like a little sick puppy and listening to all these sad behind songs 'cause she finally growing up and realizes she wants to find real love," she said, reading Dominique like a book as she pouted, but dared not tell her she was wrong because Santana was dead on today.

Returning her focus back to Kajuana, Santana continued.

"And you, missy. Let's not talk about your emotional behind. Since when have you ever been afraid to tell Michael what you were really feeling as soon as you felt that way? You have never been this sensitive as long as we have known you. Let's not forget these funky cravings of mixing pop that you *never* drink, and having a purse full of sunflower seeds and hot pickles," Santana said turning Kajuana's purse upside down and letting the contents fall out.

"Did you steal my pickles?" Dominique asked wide eyed. The stores around them never had any so Dominique had to order them offline.

Kajuana knew she was busted and decided not to even argue with her friend, because she was absolutely right. She had been seeing the signs but with everything going on in her marriage, she wanted to ignore them all. The last thing she wanted to do was have a baby and her marriage was falling apart. She was against abortions, and knew that if she was actually pregnant she would keep their child. It was just going through it without the man who vowed to be there for her wasn't something she wanted to have to deal with.

What if Michael was cheating on her? Just like her sisters knew her so well, she knew her husband the same way and on a deeper level. The love that she had for that man was nothing like she had ever experienced. Even though they had gotten together when they were young, the love never wavered and that flame had never gone out. That was until now. It still wasn't completely out, because she loved him so much, sometimes it consumed her thoughts all day long.

Somewhere within, she knew that he still loved her but there was something that was separating them and she was clueless as to what it was. Looking down on the sink, she knew that God would have to intervene and help put the pieces of His union back together.

Opening the door, she couldn't help but to smile looking into the faces of Dominique and Santana waiting on her to finish. She knew they couldn't sit still like normal people, but that smile immediately left as she released more tears. This baby was already making things complicated, and all Kajuana wanted was her husband, as her friends led her back to the front and sat with her as she cried.

-9-

Najir headed to his aunt's house for their weekly lunch date. Since he had moved back in order to take care of her because her health was failing, he made it his business to take her out often.

Mother Joyce, as she was affectionately called by everyone, wasn't his real aunt by blood, she was actually his foster mother. He had gone into the system right before his eleventh birthday and was placed with her only a few weeks later. The first day that he walked into her home, he felt nothing but love from her and her late husband Renfroe. They made it their business to make him feel at home and although he missed his mother terribly, he was glad to be with them.

His mother, Antoinette was an awesome mother to him, and even when she fell ill, she did her best to take care of him. He was an only child and they didn't have any family there, so when she had gone into a coma, no one knew who to contact to come and get him. He didn't have one of those stories where his mother was either abusive or on drugs, and that was the reason that he landed in a home but by the grace of God, even with being in the system, he never had to bounce around.

Joyce knew how he felt about his mother and she always told him that she was never there to replace his mother, but only to take care of the blessing that God had placed in her life. So when he started calling them Aunt and Uncle instead of Mama and Daddy, they welcomed it. Whatever made him comfortable was their only concern.

Uncle Renfroe was an outstanding man, and stepped in to be that father figure that Najir had never experienced. His father was never involved in his life and the sad part was that he only lived a few blocks over. Never once had he even attempted to come around and for the longest, Najir thought it was his fault. But when he went to live with Aunt Joyce, Renfroe made sure that he made up for all of the lost times.

They had one son that was grown and off on his own, and even with him coming home to visit occasionally, it was as if Najir was the only child that they ever had. The two of them would go to sporting events on the regular and they would even get out in the yard and play catch or wrestle with one another. He may have been an old man but he made sure to not let that slow him down.

With all of the fun things they did, it was the life lessons and the spiritual teachings that he got from his uncle that meant the most. Najir knew that he wouldn't be the man that he was today, had it not been for that man. The love that he had for God and the things of God, was only because he was taught at an early age.

At the time, he didn't understand the importance of being in the house of the Lord every time the church doors swung open but as he got older, it became clear. When he wanted to be out playing with his friends and being a kid, there seemed to always be either a bible study, revival, or some kind of convocation going on. He didn't even know what a convocation was, he just wanted to play. And as he drove into the driveway of the house that he grew up in, he smiled because he was thankful that they loved him enough to instill those values in him.

Since he was his own boss and today was the day he chose to be off, he was dressed comfortably. Najir could already hear Aunt Joyce fussing because of what he had on. Today he was rocking a pair of black joggers, a Carolina Panthers' hoodie, some retro Jordans, and his Panthers' snapback. That little woman knew she couldn't stand to see a grown man dressed like he was still a teen, but that was something that they would have to just agree to disagree on.

"Where's my beautiful date at?" Najir said using his key to gain access to the house. Normally Aunt Joyce would be meeting him at the door before he could get out of the car good. She told him that this was her favorite day of the week, so she made sure to be ready when he got there.

"This old coon is in here baby," he heard her say in her not so cheerful mood.

Walking towards the back of the house where he heard her voice coming from, he stopped in his tracks once he got to her bedroom door. It was almost ten in the morning and here she was still in bed. He knew that only meant one thing and that was something that he didn't want to face right now.

"Auntie, why didn't you call me?" he asked moving closer to the side of the bed that she wasn't on, and laid down beside her.

When he was younger and the thoughts of his mother would be too much for him to handle, he would stay in bed all day. Aunt Joyce would come into his room, sit on the bed beside him, and place his head in her lap. As she rubbed his head, he remembered her humming Shirley Caesar's 'No Charge' and that would make everything right in his little world. So instead of him putting his head in her lap, he pulled her close to him and placed her head on his shoulder while he closed his eyes and hummed the same song for her.

After a few minutes of the only sound being his humming, Joyce cleared her throat and began speaking.

"You know that girl likes you right?" she asked shocking him. He should have known that she would pick up on his vibes, but he still said nothing so she continued.

"And I know that you like her too."

Now this got a reaction out of Najir. Nothing on the outside suggested that he felt anything for Dominique whenever he was around her. He was never rude, but he didn't say too much to her. Not that he didn't want to.

Instead of answering her right away, he sat up and moved from the bed and walked over to the window, and asked a question of his own.

"Auntie, how do you figure I like her? I never talk to her and I've only been around her a few times."

Before she could say anything, she broke out into a coughing spell. Rushing to be by her side, Najir reached over on the nightstand and grabbed the bottle of water that was sitting on it with all of her medicines.

Taking a few sips and some deep breaths, she was able to continue what she was about to say.

"Baby, when you first laid eyes on her at church that Sunday, I saw it in your eyes. You always did think you could mask your feelings but you're my baby. Have I ever been wrong about you before when it came to anything? Especially the women," she laughed, causing him to smile because he knew that she was right.

Najir never could understand how no matter what expression he displayed, she was able to read him every time. Uncle Renfroe used to joke around and say that was the reason that he never did anything behind her back, because she would always know just by looking at him. He had to admit she was always on point.

"But how though?" he wanted to know.

"Lord, y'all men can be so slow sometimes," she chuckled before explaining. "It's in your eyes, baby. I can imagine the way that you looked at her when you saw her for the first time, was just like Adam looked when God presented Eve to him. A lot of people these days say that love doesn't happen that fast, but why can't it? Who said that there is a time limit on when you are supposed to fall in love?" she spoke looking at him, waiting on an answer.

"But if you don't know someone, how can you be in love like that?" he wanted to know. Najir was starting to become uncomfortable, so he walked over to the window again. He would always stare out of a window when he was in deep thought and needed some answers from God.

"Adam didn't know Eve but he knew God. When you are in tune with God and have a relationship with Him first, I'm inclined to believe that He already prepares us for when we meet that person. Does the relationship always work out? No. Quite a few fail, but it's not because they were wrong about their feelings, but because there was a lesson that needed to be learned for a time to come.

Those little scamboogers you used to date were just preparing you for Dominique. It's time for you to stop running from fear and step out on faith."

"Man, Auntie, you didn't see how she carried herself and all of that stuff that dude was talking about her?" Najir asked with his eyebrows furrowed and his arms crossed across the front of his body.

Joyce patted the bed beside her and waited for him to come and sit next to her. He hesitated a bit but eventually made his way to her. As soon as he sat down, she took one of his hands in hers and held it tightly. Compared to his her had was so little and fragile. Placing his other hand over that one he already held, he gently rubbed her wrinkled skin.

"Now I know we taught you to never judge someone by situations that they have gone through. Circumstances, good or bad, can cause us to react irrational at times because we are trying to make sense of it all. Dominique has been through things that no one should have to go through and no, she doesn't always make the right choices, but how many of us always make the right choices?" she asked him. She could tell that he was listening to everything she was telling him and she wanted him to hear her out before he spoke.

She had been in God's face for a long while now, about if she should be the one to tell Najir some of the issues that Dominique faced, and it took Him so long to respond that she thought maybe He wouldn't.

"Dominique has been a mother since she was just fifteen years old and not long after that, she had her second son. The man she was with was actually older than she was, so she was misled about a lot of things. Because of the pain and hurt she felt, she decided to take her own approach on her own healing instead of seeking God to help her heal.

I can't begin to tell you how many of us, me included, had we just trusted God enough to seek Him for the help we needed, could have avoided so much hell. Self-inflicted hell to me is even worse than someone else causing the hell we deal with."

Everything was making sense to him, but there was something about knowing her reputation and seeming to be okay with it that didn't sit well with him.

"All of those things that Andre said about her, never once did she try to deny it. That looks bad on her."

"Why would she deny them when she knows they are true? It's not like she doesn't know that her past choices don't now reflect good on her to people. But it's a good thing she also knows that the people have no heaven or hell to put her in. God has forgiven her and she is trying to work on forgiving herself now. And since when have some of your choices not reflected bad on you. Does that mean your heart isn't good now or you haven't turned from those ways? Don't continue to condemn someone about something God has already forgiven them for." Aunt Joyce was giving it to him real, and slowly, he was starting to let his guard down and allow his heart soften a little more towards Dominique.

His aunt was right and it caused him to think about when God told Hosea to marry the prostitute Gomer. Everyone knew her reputation but once God commanded Hosea to marry her, the love he had was unconditional and he knew that she would be unfaithful to him. Praying that Dominique wouldn't cheat on him the way Gomer had Hosea, he understood the illustration that God was giving to the people.

God lets us see through that story that even though Hosea knew his wife would be unfaithful, he still loved her no matter what. That had to take him so far out of his comfort zone to get in that relationship, but He trusted God. In spite of everything we do that goes against what God wants us to do, He still loves us. So who was Najir to judge her in any way, especially for her past?

"I get it Auntie. Lord, I need God to forgive me for how I treated her and thought of her," he said releasing her hand and placing his head in his own.

Joyce understood how he felt, as she gently rubbed her hand across his back.

"Baby, Nique has already had her body violated enough. If you go to her, be what God needs you to be for her and those babies. Don't rape her heart."

"I won't. If it's not too late and she lets me, I'll do right, I promise," Najir said, standing to his feet.

"That's my baby boy. Now give me some sugar," she laughed as she wrapped her arms around his body and he kissed her on her cheeks.

"Do you need anything before I go?" Najir asked her before he left.

"Oh no baby, I'm fine. Sarah is coming over and we are going to catch up on our show."

"What show is that?"

"*Love and Hip Hop.* Honey, that little loud girl Cardi B is a trip! Reminds me a little of Dominique when she says, 'Or whet not'. And I don't know what to do with that old buzzard Peter and those women he be bouncing off of. Lord, God need to do a mighty work in them," she said slapping her thigh like she had told the funniest joke of her life, and it even caused Najir to double over in laughter. Aunt Joyce never ceased to amaze him with some of the things she said or did.

"Alright Auntie, I'm out. I love you," he said as he walked to the front.

As he was opening the door, Mrs. Sarah was on her way up the steps with her purse in one hand, and a bag that looked like it carried containers of food in the other.

"Hey Mrs. Sarah, how are you?" he asked politely.

"Heeeeyyyyyy there baby! I see you looking handsome and whet not!" she said and made a noise that sounded like a cross between a donkey and a hyena laughing.

All he could do was shake his head and laugh at her, as he made his way to his car. This new trend of ratchet TV was even making the saints lose their minds.

-10-

"Samson, I am not doing anymore holiday themed hairstyles on you," Dominique laughed as she led him to the shampoo bowl.

If there was one thing that people could say that was positive about Samson, it was that he had some high self-esteem. Or so he made it seem. There was nothing that could be said to him that would break him down on the outside, but Dominique had learned long ago that on the inside, he was crying for some type of help. She would always drop a little nugget of wisdom that she had learned in church, or just her everyday life, and she knew that he had soaked up the information. Samson just hadn't put it to use just yet, but she knew that one day he would. She just prayed that it wasn't too late.

"Divaaa, you know Miss Samson can't come out on Easter and not serve the people what they want hunty!" he exclaimed as he dramatically sat back in the chair.

"Samson, the people don't want to see you with eggs and crosses throughout your hair," Dominique laughed as she began his treatment. The only other appointment she had today was Mother Joyce, and she prayed that Najir wasn't the one to bring her.

Every time she saw him, she got hopeful only to be let down again. It really did bother her the way he responded to her and once she expressed her feelings to her friends the other night, she felt a little better. Each day that went by and she didn't see him, she felt a little stronger. She had even made sure to schedule appointments the last two weeks so that she could have an excuse to miss Bible Study. No one else may have known what she was doing, but she knew that God, Kajuana and Santana knew.

WHY WON'T HE LOVE ME?

The little strength she had disappeared just that fast, as she looked up at the sound of the bell going off over the front door, indicating someone coming in. The moment she saw Najir walk in behind Mama Joyce, her knees got weak. Dominique didn't think anyone had noticed her reaction, but Samson did.

"I know I joke around a lot Nique, but I've been around you long enough to know when I see love in your eyes. But before you can give it to anyone else, make sure that you are capable of loving you first. You can't expect for a man to love something you don't even want to be bothered with. Now that little bit of tea was free, I'm charging you for the next cup, hunty," he said, snapping his long fingers and popping off one of his press on nails.

"Samson, I hear what you're saying, but while you are giving me advice, please take some and stop putting on those tacky press on nails. I didn't even know they made those anymore," Dominique said making sure that she got all of the shampoo out of his head before she put the conditioner in to sit a few minutes.

"Miss Samson knows a plug down at Sally's so I stay laced boo," Samson said snapping his fingers on his other hand and popping off two more nails.

A few of the women who were close by began to snicker, which caused him to show out even more. Instead of snapping in their direction and risk losing the rest of his nails, he decided to stick one of his legs straight out and dramatically cross it over the other in the opposite direction, while turning his back to them. This fool was sitting sideways in the shampoo chair with his head still facing upright.

It was something about Samson and cat suits that he loved, but he should have been loving some lotion 'cause those ankles were always a little powdery, because the leg of the one piece never did reach past the middle of his calf. Before she could say anything to him or get her laughter under control, the voice almost took her under again. She had totally forgotten that he was in her presence.

"Dominique, can I talk to you for a minute please?" Najir said as he stepped close to her.

This man was so close to her he could probably feel her heart beat. This was the closest they had ever been to one another, and she could feel all eyes on her as she tried to find her voice.

"Tika, gurrrlll, come wash this 'ditioner out my head so Sylvia can go get her groove back. Is your name Winifred?" Samson asked messing up every word he used to form that sentence.

"Fool, my name is *Deidra*, the word is *conditioner*, and *Stella* met *Winston!*" Dominique's assistant corrected Samson as he rolled his eyes at her.

"Hurry up and get your boo hunty, 'cause you know Miss Samson don't play about everybody in her hair."

Not even bothering to respond to Samson, Dominique led the way to her office in the back.

God, give me the strength to be in this heavenly creation's presence without lusting. Lord, why did you make him smell like the angel's robes? He smells so good and I know whatever you wash the angel's robes in has to smell like this man, Dominique thought to herself.

She was so far gone that she didn't even hear him until he called her name and when she turned around, she turned right into his kiss. Now she wasn't sure, but she thought that she heard a choir singing in the background and the saints break out into a full on praise break.

"As inappropriate as the thought was at church, I have been wanting to do that since I first laid eyes on you."

Dominique's face may have shown a mixture of shock and faint but on the inside, she was like, *"Ahhhhhhh come through Zaddy yassssss!"*

-11-

It was around six yesterday evening when First Lady Carla called Kajuana and wanted to schedule a meeting with her for the following day. Considering she didn't sound upset or alarming, Kajuana just figured she needed to speak with her about something concerning the church. Agreeing to meet her at one the next day, she ended the call and thought nothing else of it. She was glad that she was off so that they didn't have to reschedule it for another time.

As Kajuana headed in the direction of the church, her mind was flooded with everything that she had been going through recently. Finding out that she was indeed pregnant and thrown another monkey wrench in her life, she seriously didn't know if she was coming or going.

The moment she had seen the life growing inside of her on that monitor two days before, she knew that she needed God to work a miracle. The last thing that she wanted was to raise this baby alone, and she didn't have much time before he or she arrived.

Because Kajuana was on the heavier side and her cycle was still coming normally, she never would have guessed she was pregnant. The doctor told her that she was already heading into her second trimester, once he was able to measure the baby. As happy as she wanted to be she really couldn't, because the man that was supposed to be sharing that moment with her was now sharing his bed and life with someone else.

Kajuana never knew a pain so deep like the one she felt when that woman walked out of that hotel room that day. It was as if someone had literally reached into her chest and removed her heart, without even putting her to sleep first. Every pain she felt weakened her spirit and she wondered where she had gone wrong in her marriage.

She was a good wife and knew that she would be a good mother, but this was all too much for her. Never had Michael come home to a dirty house or an uncooked meal, and she made sure to please him in their marriage bed as much as she possibly could. What was wrong with her that he wouldn't love her like she loved him?

Tossing those thoughts to the back of her mind, she needed a clear head to deal with whatever church business First Lady needed her to do. It wasn't that she was putting church before her home life because she understood the importance of her first ministry being at home, but she needed and welcomed the distraction right now. It had been consuming so much of her lately and she just needed a break.

Walking into the front of the church, Kajuana made her way down the long hall until she got to the First Lady's study. Just as she was about to knock, the door to her Pastor's office opened.

"Hey there daughter, Lady Carla is in here waiting for you," Pastor Troy said. It took the congregation and members the longest to stop letting his name tickle them, because all they could think about when they heard his name was the rapper from Georgia whose stage name was Pastor Troy. He would even joke about it some days asking were 'We Ready' to evangelize to the people of God.

The thought tickled her and caused her to laugh on the inside and just smile on the outside. But that smile left her face so fast once she walked in the office and saw Michael sitting on the loveseat inside.

"What is he doing here?" Kajuana asked trying her best not to get upset and begin yelling. Her pressure was already a little high, her doctor expressed to her, and she couldn't afford for it to go any higher. The last thing she wanted was to put her baby in further jeopardy.

"I'm sorry that I omitted that information when we spoke yesterday Kajuana, but I was worried that had I told you Michael wanted us to meet with the both of you that you wouldn't show," she said shocking Kajuana. Why would he call a session instead of letting her know?

Well maybe that's what he had been trying to do, but she wasn't answering any of his calls or texts, so she guessed that she had forced him to go to extreme measures.

"I understand that there are some serious issues that the two of you are facing and if you want to leave, we won't force you to stay," Pastor said walking over to sit beside his wife. Three pairs of eyes looked back at her with hopeful looks in their eyes, and even if her flesh wanted to hightail it out of there, she just couldn't find it in her heart to go. They needed this and she needed some answers in order to know what she needed to do next.

The only other available spot to sit in the office was beside Michael. She said a quick prayer and asked that God kept her attitude and her hands in check. If He didn't, she would just have to repent again for jumping on her husband.

As soon as she sat down, it was as if a wave of emotions came over her. It took so much of her strength just to fight back the tears that threatened to erupt. The look on both the Pastor and First Lady's faces let her know that they felt her pain and after a quick prayer, they got started. Kajuana was so scared of what she was about to hear that it caused her to become nauseous, or either it was the baby that was making her feel that way.

"Are you and the baby okay?" Michael asked causing Kajuana to turn her head swiftly in his direction. How on earth did he know that she was pregnant?

"Dominique can't hold water in a cup," he said laughing nervously.

Kajuana couldn't wait until she saw Dominique with her watery mouth self.

"You're pregnant?" both Pastors said at the same time.

"Twelve weeks. I just found out," Kajuana said diverting her eyes to the floor and away from everyone.

"That's why I asked for the two of you to meet with us. Once I found out that my wife was pregnant, I knew that I needed to make this right. I shouldn't have messed up like I did, but my hands were tied and I panicked. Knowing that my wife is carrying my baby was like God giving me a wakeup call. I had been wanting to talk to her so bad and that was the final push that I needed," Michael said.

For the first time since entering the room, Kajuana looked into her husband's handsome face. She was missing him so much and just wanted their lives to return to normal. Depending on what he was going to reveal to her would determine their future. He was so tired and she knew it just from his weary demeanor. Not only had life been beating him up, but he had been beating himself up as well because this was all his fault. Had he just come to her in the first place, all of this could have been avoided.

The woman that he married wasn't one of those females that would hold anything over his head, as long as he was honest about it. All he had to do was communicate from the beginning, and he knew that she would have stood by him and helped him figure things out. Now he had so many secrets that they were piling up, and he gave her no other choice but to be upset about things that she didn't know of.

When he called Dominique the other day, he was actually surprised that she picked up and talked to him without an attitude. He was calling to see if she could convince Kajuana to call him but she declined. He was just about to give up when she told him that she thought it would be best for them to have a session at church. She let him know that because of her now being pregnant with his first born, they needed to have someone that was stronger in the area that they needed help in to assist them. She nor Santana were in a position to be able to give marital advice, because neither of them had been married. They hadn't even gotten a handle on just being in a relationship, let alone be able to give their opinion on marriage.

He respected Dominique even more than he already did when she told him that. It always amazed him how women or men would try and give their married friends advice when things were going wrong, when they had either never been married or couldn't keep a solid relationship long enough to gain any wisdom from those experiences. And the ones that listened to the advice was no better, because they fed into it, often times letting those opinions cause them to miss out on the blessings of God. Just because they are friends and say they have your best interest at heart, if they were willing to lead you into an area that they were not anointed to speak on then they were only in it for self-gratification and nothing more.

"So how did the two of you end up here?" First Lady wanted to know. The whole time she watched them, she could tell that the love had not gone anywhere for either of them, and that gave her hope that this could be repaired. As long as the two were honest and willing to do everything they could to make it work, then she and her husband would assist God in any way that He saw fit for them to.

"Well first of all, let me apologize. When I married you, Kay, the vow that I made to God was for real. I never meant to hurt you or put you in any type of compromising situation. What I did was selfish of me and I know that now, but at the time I couldn't see the harm in it because I didn't plan on getting caught," Michael said, turning in his seat to face his wife. He reached his hand out and placed it on her stomach and he was glad when she didn't move him away or stiffen up.

"I promise that once I get everything out, I will never do anything like this again to hurt either of you," he sighed.

Kajuana's head was beginning to swim and with each word Michael spoke, she could feel herself getting sicker by the minute. The unknown was really getting to her and it was making it so hard to focus. She just prayed that she could make it long enough for these secrets to be revealed before the contents of her stomach were.

"I'm listening," Kajuana softly spoke. Anything more would have created a disaster.

"For one, the baby that Jarmai is carrying isn't mine," he said stunning everyone in the room.

Michael had literally just made Kajuana sick and before anyone could reply, Kajuana was huddled over the trashcan that was beside her, throwing up. Both Pastor and First Lady glanced in each other's direction as Carla jumped up to grab some paper towels and a cool cloth from the bathroom. This may have been a little more difficult than either of them had anticipated. They didn't like to put a time limit on when God moved, but He was going to have to absolutely show Himself mighty and do it expeditiously.

-12-

3 Months Later

To say that being in a relationship with Cortez was one of the best feelings in life, would be an understatement. That man had enhanced Santana's life in ways that she had never thought possible. Growing up as a little girl, she could only dream of being with a person like him and even then, her dreams didn't compare. There was just one problem. She still hadn't told him what it was that she did for a living and her reasoning was nothing like it had been in the beginning.

After their first month together, Santana was almost ready to let him into that part of her life because Cortez had proved to her that he was loving her just on who she was as a person. It meant so much to her that he adored her because the feelings were definitely mutual.

They were both on the same page and feeling the same about not wanting the person they were dating to either look down on or use them for what they did or didn't have. One night when they were hanging out at his place, he expressed his feelings to her.

Cuddled up on his sofa with a fleece throw wrapped around them, Cortez felt like it was the right time to let her know what he had been feeling for her as well as what he was holding back from her.

"Babe, it's something that I need to talk to you about," he said pausing the movie.

Santana gave him her undivided attention because with the seriousness of his voice and the way his demeanor had changed she knew it was deep. Her biggest fear had been that he was about to break up with her and she just didn't know how she would handle it if he did.

"I haven't been as honest as I should have. We haven't been together that long but I do feel like I've known you all of my life. You give me this sense of peace that no other woman has ever given me. I've fallen in love with you, Tana."

Santana felt so good at that moment knowing that he was feeling her the same way she was feeling him.

"I'm so in love with you Cortez. From the day I met you it seems like you have gone above and beyond for me, and I appreciate you so much for just loving me," she said leaning over to kiss his lips.

"That's comforting to know, but I pray that you still feel the same way in a few minutes," he sighed.

"Nothing can make me change how I feel," Santana assured him.

"The only reason I haven't told you this is because I didn't want you to look down on me. I wanted you to just love me for who I am. When I went to jail it caused me to not be able to graduate and get my high school diploma. I didn't have my GED or anything so that's why I was just working over at the shop. Fixing cars had always been something I enjoyed doing and one day I want to open up my own shop. I'm tired of working for other people when God has empowered me to do more. That's why I got this," he said reaching over on the table and handing her something that looked like an IPAD cover.

When she opened it, she read silently as the realization of what she was reading hit her.

"It came in the mail today. Once I met you and we started kicking it, I realized that if I was going to eventually be your husband, I needed to take the proper steps in making sure that I could secure a future for us. So I took a crash course and got my GED."

The look on his face told Santana that he was nervous waiting on her response. She could tell that he was holding his breath as he waited.

Getting up from where she was sitting, she turned her back to him and broke out into a full on praise break! No music or anything but she was giving God His rightful praise for what He had done. She was so proud of him for making that step and there was no other way that she could express what she was feeling except by giving the highest praise.

Turning back to him, she jumped on his lap and began telling him how absolutely proud she was. For him to do that was something big, and she wasn't about to take it lightly. He deserved all of the blessings that God wanted him to have and this was only beginning.

While they hugged and he thanked her, guilt immediately filled her. It was just like the enemy to try and steal someone's joy right after God had moved. This time she couldn't even give him all of the blame though. Santana had a hand in it and she knew it. There was nothing that could make her make sense of why at that moment when he opened up, she didn't take that opening as well. That fear of what he would think was still there, so she decided to give it a little more time.

When they finally sat down, he told her how he had enrolled in a business course at the community college so that once he was able to get his business started, he would know how to run it. There were still some things that he needed to get done, but Cortez let her know that he had already applied to see if he could get a small business loan.

"I can help you with the startup costs, I don't mind," she offered.

Santana hoped that he would let her help and maybe that would wash away some of the guilt, but he didn't allow her that opportunity.

"No bae, I have to do this one myself. I want to be the one to take care of you and the children we will have some day, and this is the way that I need to do it. God already gave me clear instructions so I know that it won't fail," Cortez explained. He had made God a promise that if he was to get another chance that everything he was instructed he would do just the way he was told. No more cutting corners to get there. He was determined to get there with hard work and dedication, and with a woman like Santana supporting him while God led the way, he would be unstoppable.

That was two months ago and as each day went by, the weight of what she hadn't told him continued to weigh her down. So today she had made it up in her mind that she was finally going to let him know everything and just pray that Cortez didn't walk away from her.

***

Anxiously waiting, Santana sat at the island in her kitchen waiting on Cortez. He had conveniently called a while ago saying that he was on his way over because they needed to talk. His voice didn't sound normal to her but she just blew it off as her nerves kicking in.

Ding dong.

Getting up to head to the door, when she reached it and pulled it open, Cortez was standing on the other side looking as handsome as ever. Today he was dressed up in a nice tan suit with a white shirt under the jacket, and his tie wrapped loosely around his neck. Instead of greeting her like he did whenever they saw one another with a hug and kiss, he walked right on past her like she wasn't even there.

"Tez, you ok?" Santana wanted to know as she closed the door behind her and followed him into the living room.

Ignoring her, Cortez decided to ask her a question of his own.

"You know we have been together going on four months now and I thought things were going pretty good. I mean we had our little petty disagreements but nothing serious that we couldn't work on. Wouldn't you say, Santana?"

Whatever was bothering him was so bad that he didn't even want to make eye contact with her. She had never seen him like this and she didn't know what was going on.

"I agree but what's wrong baby?" she asked moving slowly across the room near him. All Santana wanted to do was comfort him but right then she didn't know how.

"Why is it that women can't just let men be men? Especially the good ones. You know why? I'll tell you why. It's because y'all are some selfish creatures. Everything has to be your way or no way even when we tell y'all we got it. I told you I had it!" Cortez spoke getting louder the more he talked. He wasn't making any sense and Santana was thoroughly confused.

"I don't know what you're talking about. What did you have?" Santana raised her voice.

Cortez was now up pacing the floor, as she stood there with her hands on her hips waiting on him to tell her what on God's green earth he was talking about.

"It hit me that as much time as we spend together I have never been to your place of work. Granted we are both busy while we are working and can't really talk through the day as much as we may like to, so today I decided I was going to send you some flowers or something once I left the bank.

They had called me to tell me that I needed to come down and speak with them concerning the loan I took out for my shop. Boy, I ain't never prayed so hard because I just knew that they were going to tell me something crazy like they made a mistake and needed their money back," he chuckled, but it wasn't from him being amused. It was more of a chuckle that meant he couldn't believe what was going on.

The lump in Santana's throat was so big that she was sure it looked like she had gotten a spontaneous Adam 's apple. Silently, she was praying that this was not going where she thought it was and she didn't want to open her mouth to say anything just in case he wasn't talking about what she had done. She didn't see the need to throw herself under the bus if he had no idea. Santana may have been ready to come clean to Cortez but that was only about what her profession was. Not the fact that she had paid his loan off for him.

The day he told her what he wanted to do and that he had taken a loan out for it, she wanted to help support his dream. Knowing that he wouldn't take the money from her, she decided to take matters into her own hands.

Fishing around for a little info, Santana eventually learned of the bank that he had gotten the money from. It just so happened that one of her sorors was branch manager at that particular one, and Santana immediately went in and spoke with her.

It didn't take long for her to get everything finalized for her man before she was walking out of there feeling over the moon, happy that she could do this for him. Now here she was feeling like her stepping in to help would end things between them. Still she said nothing and waited.

"Imagine my surprise when I get there and the loan officer tells me that my loan is paid off. Now I know God moves fast sometimes, but to say I was shocked would have been an understatement. As soon as she passed me those papers for me to sign, I could have cried right there.

I still didn't believe it when she told me that a company by the name of Marshall Publishing had been the generous company to sow this magnificent seed in my life, and I wanted to personally thank them.

When this lady told me that she was good friends with the CEO and she would give me the address, I was so excited. That excitement disappeared as soon as she told me that the CEO was her soror, Ms. Santana Marshall. Ha! My woman, the woman I spend every chance I can with, the woman that I had fallen in love with, the woman I wanted to make my wife and the mother of my children, had been lying to me this whole time!"

"I didn't lie to you, Tez, I just didn't tell you," Santana tried defending herself.

"That's just like telling a lie! Omitting information is just as bad and you know it. You are a freaking millionaire for Christ's sake!"

By now, Cortez was becoming completely undone and all Santana wanted to do was make it right. Had she known she was going to make it this bad for him she would have never done it, but all she wanted to do was help him.

"I was scared to tell you what I did for a living, Cortez. As long as I could remember, men would always be intimidated by how much money I made or they were only trying to use me to get what I had. I was only trying to make sure that you loved me for me," Santana tried reasoning.

"Tuh," he scoffed, "don't try to play me Santana. We both know that if that was the case you would have told me all of this the same night that I expressed to you how I felt. I bet you got a good laugh at me being just another dumb nigga, huh? I'm pouring my heart out to you about how I want to be a better person and make something of myself, and trying to be that man God has called me to be but all you see is some charity case. Give me a break," he said sounding hurt and moving towards the door.

There was no way that she wanted him to leave her, especially like this.

"Wait Cortez, don't leave. I wasn't looking at you like a charity case. I would never judge someone just because of the things they went through in life. All I did was want to help make your dream come true and be there for you. How am I supposed to sit back and let you struggle when I have the means of helping you?"

It was just like Santana to get all emotional when talking to or about Cortez. Her feelings were real and her motives were pure. She really loved this man and never wanted to hurt him.

"I'm so sorry Tez," she said trying to reach out for him, but he stepped back.

That simple movement had crushed her spirit like never before and even if he didn't say it, she felt like she had lost him.

Cortez knew she was right in her assessment and he did feel bad for how he was treating Santana, but a man's pride was known to be his downfall every time. Instead of doing what he knew he should have been, he just tried to ignore it and was failing miserably.

Kajuana and Michael weren't out of the woods just yet, but they could definitely see a clear path to the other side and they were determined to walk it together. She was now going on seven months pregnant, and the two of them were expecting a little boy. They wanted to make sure that their house and relationship was in order before little Machi made his debut.

"Hey baby, you ready?" Dominique heard Najir ask from behind her. She had only come to the house to get a shower and change of clothes so that she could go back to the hospital and be with Tricey.

It had been almost a week since Tricey had been in the hospital in more pain than she had ever been in. In order to just keep her comfortable, they had to keep her heavily sedated. Dominique was optimistic and that's really because she had Najir by her side.

Her kids loved him and that was the biggest thing for her, that Najir accepted and loved them as they were his own and the feeling was definitely mutual. At any given time, you could find him either doing something with the boys or spending quality time with Tricey, letting her dress him up for a fashion show or painting her nails. No matter what they asked of him, he aimed to please.

Snapping out of her thoughts, she checked one last time to make sure that she had everything that she needed for a few days, and they both headed out. Najir was going to drop her off at the hospital and then go and pick the boys up from school so that he could make sure their homework was done and they were fed. Since it was the weekend, Aunt Joyce had offered her babysitting services until the next day, when Santana could come and get them.

"Can you stop by the corner store for me, please, baby? I need a few snacks because the hospital vending machine be trying to get you with the prices. I could have bought a whole meal for me and you last night with the money I spent on a bag of M&M's and some water," she said as he laughed, but Dominque was dead serious.

"I got you," he told her as he pulled into the Stop-n-Go that was a block from the hospital.

Before she had a chance to get out of the car, her phone rang and it was Santana. Telling Najir to go ahead of her and that she would join him in a minute, she watched as he got out and headed inside. God knows that man was fine.

"Hey sissy! What you doing?" Dominique said answering the phone.

"You sound all chipper and stuff," Santana said and Dominique could hear the smile in her voice.

"Gurrrll, you know a good man will do it for you! Ahh—" Dominique started and stopped abruptly. She could have kicked her own behind for saying that, knowing that her friend was going through a rough time with her significant other.

"I'm so sorry Tana. I didn't mean to say it like that," she apologized.

"No need for apologies, sis. You can't stop being happy just because I'm miserable. That's not fair. What kind of friend would I be if I got mad at you about something like that? You know good and well I'm not petty like that," she said sincerely.

"I know but it came out at the wrong time. Anyway, what you up to?" Dominique asked changing the subject.

"I was just calling to check on my little princess. Have they been able to get her pain under control?" Santana wanted to know.

"Only by sedating her. Whenever my baby wakes up, she starts hollering and crying so loud. I feel so helpless and not a very good mother."

"Don't do this to yourself. You are an amazing mother Nique, and no one is blaming you for what's going on with Tricey." Santana tried her best to comfort Dominique. She may not have known what it was like to have her own child just yet, but she knew that a mother's love ran deep.

"Yes it is, because had I not been out there being fast then my baby wouldn't be going through this. This is my punishment."

Noticing Najir coming back out with bags in his hands made her realize that she was supposed to meet him inside. She did her best to quickly wipe her face and act like all was well when it really wasn't.

"What you are not going to do is make this about you right now. This has nothing to do with your mistakes or your ability of being a mother. This is all about making sure that my niece gets all of the proper care that she can so that she can live a somewhat normal life. Now shut down that pity party, put your big girl panties on, and make sure those doctors are doing what they are supposed to be doing. I will be there once I leave here to check on y'all," Santana fussed. She had gotten Dominique right on back together, just that fast.

"Okay sis. I love you and I will see you in a little bit," Dominique told her before hanging up the phone. She didn't realize that they had yet to move from the parking spot and she didn't understand why.

Turning to face Najir, she was surprised to see him looking right back in her face like he had something that he wanted to get off of his chest.

"What you looking at me like det for?" she asked as her attitude meter started rising. She knew that Santana was just being a good friend when she put her in her place, but she was still feeling a little down about not being able to do much for her child, and now Najir wanted to act like he had a bone to pick with her.

"You doing it again, huh?" he asked as he slowly pulled out into the traffic.

"Doing what?" She was not in the mood to be playing twenty-one questions with him right now.

"Putting all of the blame on you when you know that this is none of your fault, babe," he said, softening a bit and reaching over to rub her leg.

Najir was not like most men that she was used to dating. For one, he genuinely cared about the wellbeing of her and her kids. Out of all of the years she had been on the dating scene, she had ever run into a guy like that. She knew the good guys existed because of her uncle and brother, but she had never been lucky enough to experience one on a deeper level and not just in an intimate way.

That was something else that had her frustrated. She wasn't getting any. Her little buddies that she would normally have around only when she needed something sexually, had been cut off. That day that Najir came into her salon all bossed up and in her space, let her know that those other cats were no longer needed. Dominique didn't even bother telling them they were cut off. All she did was block and delete their numbers from her phone. On the rare occasion that she would see one out and he would try and holler at her, she had no problem acting like she didn't know them. A few of them cursed her out and she wanted to curse them right back, but since lashing out in public was something that bothered Najir, she did her best to keep it under control.

In no way was Najir trying to change her in a controlling way, but he wanted to help enhance who she was and get her to see her own worth. He continuously showed her that he valued her, but he wanted more than anything for her to value herself. Once she did that then he knew that no one would ever be able to make her feel less than, because she held herself to a higher standard and knew that she was royalty. To him, a woman knowing her worth was more attractive than the prettiest face and the baddest body.

"It's hard, baby, not to blame myself, but I'm working on it," she told him.

"I know and I don't mean to fuss but I hate seeing you get like that."

"Um, can you please stop rubbing my thigh like that? God knows I'm struggling over here," Dominique told him.

Once they made it official, Najir explained that he wanted them to remain celibate. If they made it to the marriage step, which he prayed it would, he wanted their first time to be like each of their first time, and be something that connects them like nothing either of them had experienced before.

At first, Dominique was looking at him sideways cause in all of her twenty-seven years of life, she had never heard of a man willingly hold off on having sex until marriage. To her that meant one of two things: he was gay or that stroke game wasn't up to par.

Dominique almost hit the floor because of his reaction when she told him her theory. He had jumped up so quick to defend his manhood, and she was weak! Najir explained that he was far from a virgin but once he made the decision to let Christ live through him, he wanted to do things right. Najir knew that the woman he married would never have the pleasure of being his first and only, but he could at least give her the new godly him, and there would be no doubt in her mind that she would ever have to share.

"Come on hot stuff, let's go check on our baby," Najir said laughing, as he parked the car in the section closest to the entrance and turned it off.

She couldn't help but to laugh at him as she followed suit and met him in front of the car. Walking hand in hand, they entered the building to go and see about their daughter.

-14-

Santana stood behind the desk inside of her office at Marshall Publishing, looking out over at the manmade lake that was located behind the building. They weren't housed in an area where she could see any bodies of water, so she created one. There was something about water that calmed her when she was stressed.

When she was a little girl, her parents couldn't keep her out of the water and every summer they made sure to take all of the girls to the beach. Vivian, Santana's mother, always told her she felt like in some way, her fascination with water was more spiritual than anything.

As she got older, she realized what her mama meant by that. There was so many miracles that Jesus performed where water was involved. He calmed the storm in the sea, He walked on water, He taught the fishermen how to fish, there was the meeting with the Samaritan woman at the well, and her all-time favorite was when He turned that water into wine! The thought of that miracle alone made her want to shout.

Laughing at herself for thinking that thought, she turned around and made her way back over to her chair. God had to be using the water as something that connected her to Him, because it was at those moments when she was lost in her thoughts that God spoke to her.

The office building was quiet since it was a Friday, and she welcomed the silence. This was where she ran her day-to-day operations and even some of her authors had offices there for when they needed to get out of their homes to write. Very rarely would there be any more than ten authors there at a time, because most of them worked from home so it was usually just her assistant, the HR department, her PR team, and a few other people here and there. All in all, Santana was grateful for God blessing her with this opportunity to not only be successful, but to help others become successful as well. There was just one problem, there was no one to share her success with.

Santana knew that God had intended for her to have a husband and a family, and deep down she still felt like Cortez was the one she was supposed to have all of that with. She just didn't know if he felt the same way anymore. They still hadn't said the words that they were no longer an item, but for Santana, actions were speaking louder than words.

Finally deciding to call it a day so she could head over to the hospital and see her niece, she got up and started to gather her things when her phone rang.

"Hello?"

"Hey baby girl, how are you? You forgot about your old folks?" her father spoke from the other end.

"Speak for yourself Phillip, 'cause I am not old. You may be old but baby, I'm still poppin'! Hey my pretty girl!" Santana's mother sassed.

"You sure are my little tenderoni," Philip agreed causing Santana to laugh out loud.

Her parents were some characters, and for as long as she could remember they had had been that way. That upcoming November they would be celebrating thirty-seven years of marriage. They were two of the best examples of how to make a marriage work and she wanted to have that so bad.

"So what's going on Daddy?" she asked trying to get his attention. There was no telling what her parents were doing because all she could hear was giggling from the other end.

"I just wanted to see if you have patched things up with my son-in-law yet?" he asked, referring to Cortez.

The first time that they met him they fell in love with Cortez, and vice versa. Her mother was smitten by his good looks and even joked about hurrying up and marrying him so that Santana could give her some grandbabies. Her brother hadn't been able to give them any and they treated

Dominique's kids like they were their grandchildren, but Santana knew that they wanted a few from her.

"Not yet, Daddy," she sighed.

"What are you waiting on?"

"Why do I have to be the one to do it? I already apologized for not telling him about what I do for a living and explained why I hid it from him. He needs to apologize to me for being judgmental," Santana fussed.

"That's not what I'm talking about and you know it," he said.

"Unt uh, give me that phone 'cause this don't make no sense. You trying to pity pat her and she needs it straight with no chaser!" Santana heard her mother say. This was not about to be something that she wanted to hear but if she was to keep it real with herself, then she would know that it was needed. But in regular Santana fashion, she was going to be as stubborn as she could for as long as she could.

"Now you listen here, little girl. That man loves you but you being too selfish to even realize it. Yes, he waited a while to tell you about his education status and that he wasn't bringing in a lot of money right now, but he was embarrassed. Did you even take the time to find out if there was a reason for his embarrassment?" Vivian went in.

"N—" Santana began only to be cut off by her mother.

"Did I ask you to talk? You better hush until I ask you a question," she said.

Santana wanted to laugh but she knew better. This was always how her mother fussed. Asking a question then when she would answer it, she was told not to talk. What was the point in asking if she didn't want an answer?

Vivian continued. "No you didn't because you were only worried about you and what you were feeling. Little selfish behind. Instead of you being concerned about him like he has been all this time about you, then you wouldn't have gone down to that bank and paid that loan off."

Now Santana was confused. The whole reason she paid the loan for Cortez was because she loved him and knew that he wanted better.

"But Mommy, I—" Santana tried again.

"Philip, did you drop this child on her head when she was a baby? Did I not just tell her behind to hush. Get this here phone 'cause she 'bout to make me curse and I just left from that prayer meeting."

Santana waited as her mother passed the phone back to her father and hoped that instead of him fussing at her too, he would just fill her in on what she was missing.

"Baby girl, what your mother is trying to say to you is that had you really been listening to what he was telling you about his plans and what he wanted to do, then you would have known that it was something that he needed to prove to himself.

There may have been a time when all people kept telling him was that he would never be anything or he would never be successful. Now that he is older and learning to trust God more, he wanted to prove this to himself. Getting his GED was the first step, deciding to open this business was the second, and him paying that loan off himself would have been huge to him. Nothing means more to a man than him being able to be a provider.

I already liked the young man when I met him because I could see the light of the Lord shining bright in him. But after finding out what he did, that just made me respect him even more and I know that he would make an awesome husband and be an even better father to my grandbabies. You get what I'm telling you baby?" Philip explained.

The way her father had just broken everything down to her made her feel even worse. He was absolutely right. She was thinking so much of herself that she didn't even take the time to listen to what Cortez was telling her. He didn't need anything from her but her support, as he took care of business like a man was supposed to. Now he felt like she was making him a charity case by flaunting her money around, and that couldn't have been further from the truth. Santana realized that she needed to fix this and make it right. She just hoped that it wasn't too late for them.

-15-

After Santana hung up with her parents, she made sure that all of her systems were shut down and the office locked up. All of her appointments had been taken care of, and she made sure to clear her schedule until the end of the month.

Right after she attended the AAMBC Literary Awards the following weekend, Santana would be on her way to Miami for two and a half weeks. Some time alone so that she could get her thoughts together was definitely needed. Things in her life were crazy and it was time to regroup before she lost her mind.

She said goodbye to the night janitor, Mr. Tommy, and headed out to her car that was in the front. It was a little after two in the afternoon and the growling of her stomach reminded her that she had missed lunch. Instead of stopping, she figured she would just grab something from the hospital cafeteria before going up the stairs to see her pooh.

Very seldom could Santana find a good parking space, so she hoped today would be a little easier and it wasn't packed. Pulling out of the lot and hitting the hands free device on her steering wheel, she placed a call to Cortez. It felt like her heart was about to jump out of her chest because she didn't know how this conversation was about to go. She had hoped for the best but who knew how he would receive her.

The phone rang almost six times before he picked up, and the tone of his voice let her know that he was already aggravated. She didn't know if it was because of her or if he was just having a bad day. Santana almost wanted to chicken out and hang up, but she was scared that if she did that then he might not even call her back to see if it was an accident or not. That would crush her even more than she was at the moment.

"Yea, wassup?" Cortez answered on his end.

"Um, hey Cortez, how are you?"

Santana's nerves were so bad and she knew that he could hear her voice shaking but he wasn't moved.

"I'm straight," was his simple reply.

"Well I was wondering if we could meet up and talk," she said as she held her breath waiting on him to respond.

It sounded like he was moving around until the background noise died down.

"I don't know man. I need to check my schedule. I got a lot of stuff coming up and I just don't know. You can't say what you need to say over the phone?" Cortez questioned.

Santana could feel the tears welling up in her eyes and her throat tightening, when he didn't agree with meeting her. She didn't even know what to say at the moment and wished that she hadn't even called him in the first place.

"No, it was something that needed to be said in person but never mind."

"Aight then," he said quickly, not even bothering to let her finish, and hung up. As soon as the two consecutive beeps notified her that he was no longer on the line, the tears fell. It was at that moment that she felt like she had lost him for good and, it hurt unlike anything she had ever experienced.

When she broke up with Tavion, her first love, when she was in the eleventh grade, she thought that was the worst thing ever. Right then, there was nothing that could compare to what she was feeling, knowing that the man who she had fallen in love with didn't want her and it was all her fault.

Her mother was right when she said that she was selfish and only thought about herself. It was that way of thinking that has always gotten her in trouble. Santana wished she had prayed about what she was going to do for Cortez before she did it. That was where she messed up.

Sighing at the sight of the parking lot being full, she knew this was going to be a task in itself trying to find somewhere to park. Instead of parking in the front, Santana thought about parking around by the cafeteria. Since she had already planned to get something to snack on, that made a little more sense. Sometimes there wouldn't be too many spots taken up after the lunch hour was over, so she drove around to try her luck, although she wasn't having much of that lately.

Luckily, there were actually a few spots, so she whipped into one and grabbed her stuff. Hitting her alarm, she began to walk towards the door when she noticed a car that looked like Cortez's. Shaking it off, she laughed to herself. This man was consuming so much of her thoughts that she was thinking she was seeing him everywhere. There really wasn't a reason for him to be there and if he was there to check on Tricey, then Dominique would have told her.

It wouldn't have been unusual for him to be there because while they were dating, he had taken a liking to all of her kids and even let them call him Uncle Tez. There were a few times that he stopped by and either Dominique or Kajuana would let her know just in case she was on the way and didn't have time to call them first.

The main cafeteria was already closed for the day, but they had a little café and grill inside to accommodate the people that either worked past the main lunch hour or the visitors that came in all throughout the day.

Looking up at the menu to see what she wanted, nothing on it sounded pleasing to her. Just as she had decided on getting a lemonade and a fruit parfait, she heard laughing coming from behind her. It wasn't the laughter that made her want to cry again, it was what the person said.

"Cortez, your grandmother was right, you are something else," the woman laughed.

Whipping her head around and almost giving herself whiplash, she turned right into the face of Cortez. When he saw her, the smile that he had immediately left his face and his eyes bounced around the room. Santana looked at him for just a few seconds before placing her items back down, and walked off towards the hall leading to the elevators.

"Tana, wait!" Cortez called after her. Santana almost melted when she heard him call her name. Lately when she saw him, it was either her full name or that one time that he crashed her face and called her 'Sister' at church.

Instead of turning around, she kept her head straight because she knew that if she turned to see him, he would see her crying, and she was tired of him having that effect on her.

"Still being selfish and stubborn I see," Cortez snapped. This caused her to turn around. She didn't care if her makeup was running and she looked like a mad woman.

As soon as he saw her, he wished that he hadn't been so harsh. It was killing him on the inside that they had gotten to this point, but here they were.

"I'm not being stubborn or selfish right now. I call you so that we could meet and talk and you tell me that you have to check your schedule and hang up on me because I don't want to talk about it over the phone. Then I walk in here and see you all up in the next chick's face. So no Cortez, I'm not stubborn, I'm hurt. And even more so because I hurt you. I wanted to make things right and fix what I messed up between us, but I guess I'm too late," Santana cried before walking off.

As bad as Cortez wanted to go to her and wrap his arms around her and say that everything would be alright, he just couldn't bring himself to do it. He knew that she was hoping that he would come behind her but he didn't. Letting her go was the hardest thing to do right then, but he had to.

***

When the elevator doors closed, Santana's body shook as she cried out. It was one of those cries that came from the bottom of her soul and as it traveled up her body, the closer it got to being released the louder it was. The tears were coming so fast and so hard that all she could do was drop to her knees. She didn't even care that at any moment those doors would open again and that someone would see her in that condition. Nothing mattered.

"Oh my God, sis, what's wrong?" Santana heard Dominique say as she rushed over to her.

Dominique was on her way downstairs to get something to drink when the elevator opened and she saw her friend balled up on the floor. Initially she thought that someone had attacked her and that was the reason she was in this state, but then she saw that Santana's purse was by her side and her phone was hanging loosely in her hand.

"I've lost him for good," Santana said before she continued to cry, even louder this time. There was something about being around someone else when they asked you what was wrong, that made a person cry harder.

"Come on, let's go in the room first and then we will talk," Dominique said as she helped her up the best that she could, and started walking towards Tricey's room.

When they reached the door to the room and went inside, Santana didn't even realize that Granny was in the room.

"Jesus, what's happened to my baby? Are you alright child?" Cortez's grandmother asked her.

Santana hearing her voice made her shoot her head up and run over to where Granny was sitting on the small sofa chair.

"Shhh, it's alright baby. It's going to be okay," she told Santana as she wrapped her arms around her shoulders and held her close.

Being that Santana's parents no longer lived in Illinois and had moved down to Texas once her father retired, it was good to have this mother figure in her life when she needed it. Santana knew that she could always call her mother when needed, but there were those times when she just needed a hug, and they were too far apart. Once she met Cortez, she and Granny had become close. Even when the big blow up happened between the two, Granny made it very clear that she wanted Santana to remain in her life. So whenever Cortez wasn't around, Santana made sure to stop by and check in, or sit with her at least three or four times a week. It was still hard to be around her knowing that at any time Cortez could pop up.

"Granny, he don't love me no more," Santana cried as she held on to Hattie tighter.

Dominique almost laughed and had to catch herself because Santana sounded just like Taraji P. Henson when she played Yvette in *Baby Boy*. She could see the scene clear as day, as Jodi passed their son to Yvette in the pouring rain and slammed the door. Once she got back into her friend's car, that was the same thing that Yvette told her.

Getting lost in the movie, Dominique thought about watching that once she got home. That was one of her favorite movies of all times, and it had been a minute.

"You can't lose something that hasn't been lost baby," Granny said to her.

Now Dominique wasn't a relationship expert, but she was pretty sure that when a man walked out and didn't want to be bothered with a woman, then that meant they were over. That kind of thinking must have been during the 50's, or she was just trying to be nice to Santana, but lil' buddy was gone.

It was a shame too, because Cortez and Santana made one nice looking couple, and she knew that the love they had for one another ran deep. There was a little hope that she had stored away that maybe they could get themselves together, but that hope went straight out the window as soon as the door to the room opened.

In walked Cortez with a short, blond hair, blue eyed woman in tow. See, had this been any other location, Dominique would have gone off. But her baby was in that bed and this was not the time. Cortez didn't know how Tricey had just saved him 'cause he would have gotten slapped for pulling a stunt like this.

The look on Cortez's face let him know that this was all bad, but there was nothing that he could do about it. As soon as

Santana saw him, she grabbed her purse and went to kiss Tricey on her head.

"Wait baby, don't go, this needs to be resolved," Granny said.

"I can't do this Granny," Santana replied. She had barely gotten herself together and here she was about to lose it some more.

"Sis, wait, let me walk you out," Dominique said walking towards her.

"No. You knew he was here and you didn't even call me to let me know. And he was with another woman. Come on Nique, we were supposed to be better than this."

"Hold on now, you know no one comes before you, especially some broad that I don't know. I didn't even know that Cortez was here. You know I would have called you," Dominique defended herself.

"You're right, I'm sorry. Call me later," Santana apologized and Dominique simply nodded her head.

Before leaving out of the door completely, Santana looked over to where Cortez was standing not saying a word. He didn't even try and say anything to comfort her. Without anything further, Santana walked out and headed towards the elevator.

She knew what it was that she needed to do. Not even bothering to go home and pack, she got in her car and headed to the airport. It was time to leave for a while and she needed to do it fast.

-16-

"Boy, if I was still a cusser I would cuss you something terrible right now!" Granny said trying her best to get out of her seat. She had to rock back hard and push forward about three times before she could get off of the chair because it was so low, but once she did it was on and poppin'.

Dominique wanted to pull out her phone and record this event and put it on Pay Per View 'cause it was about to be the fight of the century. All of her money was going on Granny.

Lord, forgive me, this is not the time to be making jokes, even if you are the only one who can hear me, Dominique thought to herself. She was so weak on the inside and it was so inappropriate.

The part that wasn't funny though was that Santana had left so upset and there was nothing that she could do for her girl at the moment. She made a mental note to stop by there before she went home to check on her.

"Man Granny, why you mad at me? I didn't do anything to that woman. Just like always she jumping to conclusions and only thinking about herself," Cortez said sucking his teeth.

"You may not be a child anymore but suck your teeth again and see what happens," Granny told him.

She was a feisty little thing and Dominique loved it. Dominique hoped that when she was that old that she would still be able to check her a few people if they got out of line.

"I'm just saying that I don't owe her anything. I tried to be open with her but she continued to lie, even when she had the opportunity to do the same," Cortez defended himself.

"And you didn't lie to her either?" Granny asked. Dominique knew exactly where she was heading. There had been many times that Dominique wanted to ask him the same thing, but God just wouldn't let her intervene.

"I mean, I did hold out on telling her what I had gone through because I didn't want her to look down on me, but once I fell in love with her and how she treated me, I wanted her to know," he said.

"Hmm. You know what? You are a handsome but dumb little pot," Granny said causing both Dominique and the blond bombshell to both giggle. They all had forgotten she was still in the room until that moment.

"I'm sorry, Marissa, for holding you. Thank you for showing my grandson exactly what I needed at home. I will see you next week," Granny told the woman Dominique now knew as Marissa.

Marissa was real pretty but she wasn't her friend Santana. Dominique was Team Tana all day long and if Cortez thought that they would be alright with him bringing his little side thing around them, then he was in for a rude awakening. True enough the men in all of their lives had grown pretty close, but that didn't mean Marissa would be invited to any function they had. And how was it that Cortez had already moved on but had yet to officially break things off with Santana? That was something she was going to have to get out of Najir and that would be like pulling teeth out of a hungry lion's mouth.

Najir had told her too many times to just be there to comfort Santana but not try to fix anything. This was hard for her because they had always been there for each other in any way possible, but she was trying this submissive thing First Lady told her about. She didn't know how long this was gonna last but for now she would try.

"Alright, Mrs. Hattie. Cortez did you need to get my number just in case you needed anything?" Marissa asked him.

This struck Dominique as odd because if they were together then why didn't he already have her number?

"Oh no baby, if there is anything that I need I can call you or call the nursing agency and speak to the director myself," Granny expressed.

Granny was that deal! Without even breaking her smile, she let Marissa know to back off of Cortez, or she would be making a call to the director of her job. That was a classy piece of shade Granny threw and she was going to have to ask for her to teach her how to do it.

Besides that, it made Dominique feel better knowing that she would be able to relay this little bit of information to Santana a little later.

"Yes ma'am," Marissa said embarrassed as she walked out of the room.

Shaking her head, Granny walked back over to her seat before speaking again.

"Santana saw you with Marissa before she came in here, didn't she?" Dominique asked Cortez now that things were adding up.

Without a word, Cortez nodded his as he made his way over to the window. He needed a body of water to calm his mind. Something about water always eased him and he never knew why. Closing his eyes, he interlocked his fingers and placed his hands on the top of his head. Cortez took a long deep breath and let it out hard. He was hurting and just like a man, his pride didn't want anyone to know.

"Tezzy, why didn't you tell her then so she wouldn't assume anything? That girl is broken already and that just made it worse," Granny said sounding like she was finally calming down a little bit.

"You call him Tezzy? Heyyyy Tezzy!" Dominique said at the wrong time. Both Granny and Cortez turned to mug her 'cause she just didn't know when the right time was to jump in nor did she care.

"Whet?" Dominique asked like she didn't know what she had done wrong. She thought the name was funny.

Granny pointed her long finger to the chair that was in the corner, indicating that Dominique needed to go sit her behind down. Dominique may have been grown and was flip at the lip but she knew who to play with and who not to, and Granny definitely wasn't the one. Poking her lips out, she crossed her arms across her chest and sat her butt right on down.

"I didn't tell her because once again, she was only thinking about herself and started going off on me. Talking about how she asked if we could talk and I told her I had to check my schedule, but I was up here with someone else. She didn't even give me time or the opportunity to tell her that Marissa was your nurse," he said like he was justified.

"God, slap him down ret nie in the mighty name of Jesus 'cause he so slow," Granny closed her eyes and said. Dominique wanted so badly to laugh 'cause Granny was going in, but she wouldn't even play with her life like that. Mess around and be in a bed beside Tricey, so she just watched.

"You mean to tell me that she asked to meet with you and you told her no, then you got the nerve to be mad that she reacted like she did?" she asked.

Cortez simply shrugged his shoulders.

"Why are you really mad?" She asked him the question that had yet to be asked. Granny had heard both sides of the story and tried to give only a little advice because she wanted them to figure things out on their own, but obviously they couldn't do it.

"Honestly, it's not even about her not telling me about what she did for a living. We could have worked past that. I'm mad because I told her that I wanted, no, I *needed* to handle this business on my own. I always hear that I need to put my faith in God and let Him show me who He is in my life. I told her all of this and what did she do? She went right down there and paid something for me that I didn't ask her to."

Now that Dominique was really listening to what Cortez was saying, she was understanding a little bit more about why he felt the way he did. She didn't think it was right how he was treating Santana but she could understand his reasons.

"Come here Tezzy," Granny said before both she and Cortez looked at Dominique. Holding her hands up in surrender, Dominique said not one word.

Doing as instructed, Cortez went and sat beside his grandmother while she reached in her big brown purse. Dominique knew that if they went to the movies together, they could pack a serious lunch in that bag and not get caught.

Pulling out her bible, she flipped through the pages until she got to the book and chapter she was looking for. Granny didn't know it but Dominique was all ears. She knew that something good was about to be said and no matter how rowdy she got or how many jokes she told, Dominique loved to hear the word of God and the wisdom that came from it.

She had learned that not all of the time will God speak directly to us, but He would use other people or situations to speak to us. That was why we must always be in touch with Him to know when He spoke.

"Here, read this," Granny told Cortez as she passed him the book.

"Luke chapter six verse thirty-eight says, 'Give and it shall be given. Good measure, pressed down, shaken together and running over, shall men pour into your bosom'," he read.

Granny could see that it wasn't registering in his mind just yet, so she decided to help him out a little bit.

"I'm a firm believer that God will use people to bless others in tremendous ways," she said.

"I know He will that's why I trust Him now more than ever," Cortez said.

"Do you really?" Granny asked him with one of her eyebrows raised. She had this amused look on her face that Dominique didn't understand.

"Yeah," Cortez replied.

"So why could you not receive the answer to the prayer that you brought before God? The one where you asked for Him to help you to start your own business so that you could be the provider Santana needed?" she wanted to know.

"I'm not understanding. When God blesses me, I will know it," Cortez said, finding himself getting upset. He wasn't necessarily mad at Granny, but he was just tired of the roundabout. He wanted to know what she was getting at.

"You just read in that scripture that God will use *men* to pour into your bosom. God sent you exactly what you asked for, and Santana was the one to bless you. She poured into you and didn't ask for anything in return. Her only mission was to make sure that you got to where it was that you wanted to go. But you were so caught up on thinking that she was throwing her money around, or making you out to be a charity case, that you didn't even see the double portion of a blessing that God had given to you.

Santana is to be your help mate. That means that she is there to be your helper. No, you aren't married yet, but if that is where you know God is sending you, then be glad that He sent you someone who isn't looking to judge you because of where you have been, but wants to help you get to where she knows you can go. That woman was not trying to make you feel less of a man, but you were being selfish and thinking of only yourself. She, on the other hand, was putting you first.

Men have to learn that it is ok to receive help from people and if that person just so happens to be a woman, it doesn't make you less of a man. You can still be the provider and cover your family baby. Do you understand what I'm telling you?" Granny finished.

When she got done, it was like Dominique and Cortez's eyes were open and they both understood what she was saying.

Holding his head down, Cortez nodded his head.

"I messed up big time," he said.

"Yeah you did that nie," Granny said causing them all to laugh. "But you can turn this mess into a message."

"Mommy?" Tricey said making everyone jump up and run to her side.

"My baby!" Dominique said trying her best not to cry.

"Go get the nurse, Tezzy," Granny prompted as he ran out of the room.

"Can I go home now?" Tricey smiled

"Are you in any pain princess?" Dominique asked.

"No ma'am. Can I have some Starbursts?" Tricey asked making her mother laugh. That little girl knew that she loved her some Starbursts.

"Yes baby, as soon as we go home I will get you some."

"Okay. Are my brothers and Daddy here?" Tricey wanted to know just as the doctor and nurse rushed in.

"No baby, but while Dr. Thompson makes sure you're okay, I will go call them and tell them to come see you alright?"

Instead of answering her mother, Tricey just smiled as they walked out into the hall. Granny told her how happy she was that Tricey was now awake and seemed to be doing better. She promised to come and check on her again tomorrow, and once she went home. It was getting close to the time to take her medicines and she wanted to be home before they kicked in, making her sleepy.

They all said their goodbyes as Dominique called to give her sons and her boo the good news. God was still in the blessing business.

-17-

Kajuana sat on her couch and rubbed her big belly as she felt her baby boy kick. Michael was on his way home with dinner and she couldn't wait to eat. In just a few short months, she and Michael would be welcoming their first child together. It was going to be a long journey but she knew that the end results would be so worth it, as long as they kept God first.

Shaking her head, she thought back to how everything unfolded.

***

After they met with Pastor and First Lady that day and Michael started off telling her that the woman she had caught him with wasn't carrying his child, Kajuana flipped. Before she knew it, First Lady was trying to pry her hands from around his neck and Pastor was trying to help her. It was so bad that they had to end the session and reschedule.

For almost two weeks straight, Kajuana ignored Michael and went to stay in a hotel. She didn't want to be a burden to anyone and she really just wanted to be alone. The only time she would go out was when she needed food or hygiene products. Because she was broke, Santana made sure that she had more than enough money to do whatever she needed. She had even given Kajuana one of her bank cards so that she could have full access to funds and Dominique made sure to put money in there for her as well. Kajuana told them that they didn't need to do that but they weren't trying to hear it. No matter how much she fussed or told them she was okay, Kajuana was glad that they had her back.

Then one day while they were out together, Michael popped up. The looks on Santana and Dominique's faces let her know that the only one surprised by him being there was her. Kajuana's body had been sore so she couldn't move as fast as she normally would when she tried to get up to leave.

WHY WON'T HE LOVE ME?

"Kay, please, just hear me out baby," Michael pleaded. There was nothing that she wanted to hear from him right now but she had no choice. All three of them looked pitiful and she knew the longer that she fought having the conversation, the longer it would take for her to move on.

"Fine." Was all she said as she sat back in her seat.

Santana and Dominique got up to give them some privacy and Michael wasted no time pleading his case.

"I know the last time we talked things went left. When you left, Pastor explained to me that maybe I shouldn't have started the way that I did without explaining the other stuff first.

I thought that you had noticed the bulge of Jarmai's stomach and being that we were at the hotel you were thinking that was my baby," he said.

"No Michael. I never even paid attention to her stomach. I was more focused on why my husband was there with another woman who acted like she knew who I was, but I had no clue as to who she was," Kajuana said feeling frustrated. Never would she have thought that she would have to be sitting here having a conversation like this with the man that she married.

"That's because she does know you. I talk about you all of the time. The whole reason I was even involved with her in the first place was because of you."

"Me?" Kajuana was shocked to say the least. How on God's green earth was her husband with another woman? She was a good wife and took care of all of his needs so that he would never have to look anywhere else for what she was lacking. Could she have been wrong all of this time? It didn't matter now anyway because obviously she was missing something.

"I don't mean it like that, babe. You have done everything right for as long as I can remember, and on the times that something wasn't right, you owned it and we worked through it. I lost my job back in November, Kay," Michael revealed as he put his head down.

Kajuana was floored. Michael had been getting up and pretending like he was going to work like he normally, did and he was doing it for at least four months before the day that she caught him at the hotel.

"That was four months ago! What were you doing every day then when I thought you were going to work?" she said raising her voice. A few of the people that were in close proximity looked over in their direction and she had to realize she was out in public. Dominique was the one who didn't care where she popped off, but Kay did and here was not the place.

"I know, and if I could take it all back I would. Please believe me when I say that I wasn't cheating on you. Since we have been together, I have never given another woman any part of me, especially my heart," he said reaching out to grab her hand.

Kajuana tried to pull her hand back, but he wouldn't allow her to. He needed to feel his wife and he didn't care how much or how little of her body it was; he yearned for her. Once she stopped fighting him and gave in by keeping her hand in his, he finally let her know what was really going on.

"I started back smoking because I felt like that would ease my mind some. Not having a job and being able to provide for my wife was something that no man wants to face, and instead of coming to you I wanted to fix it. It seemed like every job that I applied for I was either over qualified or they just weren't hiring.

After a couple of weeks, I was running out of options so that's when I started taking money out to gamble with. I knew it wasn't right but I didn't know what else to do. The first few times I won, I was able to put the money back so that you wouldn't be able to tell, but then I kept getting deeper and deeper into it. The more I gambled the more I lost. So I tried something else.

I got involved with this dude I knew around the way that gave people loans when they needed it."

"You mean a loan shark?" Kajuana cut him off. She had heard how ruthless those type of people were, and she couldn't believe that Michael had gotten tied up in something like that.

"Yeah. With your hours at the hospital getting cut some days, and me not having work at all and spending all of our savings, I was scared that we would end up out on the streets. I couldn't have that.

When I was telling you that I would make all of the payments on everything, it was because I had already paid most of our mortgage off and all of the other bills were paid up.

But then I was starting to get behind on the payments to him. I figured that once I got the money from Neko, it would buy me some time to get back to work and I could pay him back. It's just that a job didn't come through so I needed a way out. I prayed and I prayed for something to open up and that's when I found out about the other account." He stopped. Michael felt her tense up when he said that and he slid closer to her while never taking his eyes away from her.

"Go on, Michael," Kajuana said sounding defeated.

"It was just the amount of money I needed in order to be rid of Neko for good, so I took it. I was on my way home to tell you what I had done when you caught me coming out. I felt defeated, even though I knew that I didn't have anything connecting me to Neko anymore. I felt defeated because I hadn't been honest with you."

This was a lot to take in and Kajuana knew that it sounded farfetched, but she also knew her husband. And sitting there looking into his eyes while he confessed his faults to her, she knew he was telling her the truth. She just had one more question.

"What about the hotel charges, Michael?" she asked him. Yeah, he had laid everything out on the table but if that was all true, what were the hotel rooms for and why was he there with that woman?

"Neko is into so much stuff that he makes sure to cover his tracks. Whenever I had to pay him, he would make sure that his wife, Jarmai and I met at the hotel. He said that it would look like we were having some type of affair, if anything, and I was the one that had to pay for the room. If anything happened, nothing *could be tied back to him because no one could say that they ever saw him." Michael finished.*

"I thought you didn't love me anymore," Kajuana whispered as her eyes watered.

"Oh baby, no. Please forgive me, because the last thing that I ever wanted to do was make you doubt my love for you. When I married you, I made a vow to God to love you forever and if you give me the chance, I will do my best to make this up to you. I know I was wrong but I only wanted the best for us, but I went about it the wrong way. I can admit I messed up but I never want you to feel like any of this was your fault."

"I love you so much, Michael. Please talk to me if anything like this ever happens again. I am here for you no matter what. We are a team and come hell or high water, I don't want to win with anyone but you," Kajuana told him, reaching out to him.

It felt so good being back in her husband's arms and feeling like there was nothing blocking her heart anymore. She was so close to walking away but she couldn't do anything but bless God for keeping them together. There was rebuilding that needed to be done but she was in it for the long haul.

***

Michael walked into the house breaking her from her thoughts and immediately the smell of the Mexican food that she was craving hit her nostrils. He couldn't help but to laugh at her trying to get up and wobble towards him to grab the bag out of his hand.

"I can't get a kiss first? Man that's cold," he said smiling.

"Awww Daddy, I'm sorry." Kajuana leaned in like she was going to give him a kiss and as soon as he closed his eyes, she snatched the bag.

"You know what? I'm gonna let you slide for now but I know later I better get a kiss."

"You can have anything you want baby. As soon as I feed your son."

"Oh word? Well feel my lil' man and hurry up," he said laughing.

The two of them sat in the living room, eating their meals and talking about each other's day. He told her how he was liking the new job and Kajuana couldn't have been happier.

Come to find out, Najir owned a construction company. Since he was new to the area, he had been looking to hire people. Once everything had come out about Michael losing his job, Dominique suggested he go and talk to Najir. The minute he walked in, he was hired on the spot. Najir felt like with his experience of the area and his background, he would be a big asset to his company, and he already knew what was going on. He was glad to help Michael and Michael was glad for the help. He made a promise to himself that he would never let his pride get in the way, ever again.

It was finally time to stop playing and get his grown man on, and every chance he got he made sure to thank God each and every day for helping him to get it right.

-18-

Dominique had just finished her last client for the day, and she was sitting there talking with Samson until Najir came to pick her up from the shop. He was having her car detailed so he had dropped her off that morning. The more she spent time with him, the more she thanked God for her blessing.

They had been going strong and even with the lack of sex, Dominique felt like they were on such a deeper level. Once they did finally take it there, she knew that it was going to blow the both of their minds. No it wasn't priority right now, but she couldn't wait to give Najir something that no man had ever gotten, and that was her heart to go along with her body. She now knew her worth and it was all thanks to Najir helping her to see that.

"Earth to my boo!" Samson said bringing her out of her thoughts. No matter what Dominique was doing, whenever she thought of the goodness of her man and all that he has done for her through God, she basked in those thoughts.

"Yes ma'am," she said, giving Samson and his getup her full attention.

In true Samson fashion, he was rocking another horrible 'She by Samson' ensemble. He cracked Dominique up when he told her he was going to start a clothing line because it was too many people that needed his expertise in the fashion world. She didn't know who those people were, but she was sure if they needed his expertise they had to have been blind. Samson couldn't dress a poodle.

Today he was wearing a lime green high-low shirt, some dark purple stretch pants, and some white patent leather kitten heels. Homeboy thought he was giving life, but failed to realize that he was killing everybody that saw this getup. This fool had the nerve to have a prayer shawl wrapped around his shoulders knowing good and well he was not about to pray. If he did, he seriously needed to ask God for two new eyes because the ones he had now told him that he was fly.

"So what's going on with Miss Santana, hunty? Did she get back with that foine piece of man, Carlito?"

This fool.

"Samson, for the thousandth time the man's name is Cortez, and you know I don't pour my sister's tea for them," Dominique reminded him.

"That must mean no. Well look, tell him if he needs someone to hold him down I am always available. Chile, ain't no need for him to be lonely at night," Samson said with his lips tooted up as he crossed his legs.

Samson's pants may have been long enough to cover his legs so Dominique couldn't see his ashy ankles, but those feet were a different story.

"Um, do you have on some sheer white stockings?" Dominique asked looking down at it feet.

"Girl no, it is too hot for the doll to be wearing some stockings."

There weren't many people in the salon but the few that were, all got weak.

"What's so funny?" he asked not catching on to what was so funny.

"You know boy, when I go to church Sunday I'm going to ask them to take up a love offering for you. Better yet, we gonna get a care package together with some lotion, a full set of nails, a fashion book for dummies and a clue, because you have none," one of our regulars, Tanechea said, and that caused everybody to fall out again.

All Samson could do was suck his teeth. He was not about to get into it with any of these silly broads and risk messing up his new hairdo. Dominique finally got herself together and turned around to start getting her things packed up and ready to go. She knew that Najir would be there in a few minutes to get her, and she wanted to be ready so that she could get just walk out when it was time.

The area in which her station was located in the shop was right behind the receptionist station, so in order to see her you would have to walk around the wall. Dominique hadn't been back there but a few minutes, when she heard the bell chime indicating someone had entered. Thinking it was Najir, she didn't stop what she was doing because he knew where to find her. Just as she was about to unplug her irons, she picked them up only to drop them because of what she heard.

"Hey baby, you ready to go?" the man said.

"Yes daddy, you already know," Samson said.

The devil is a lie! Dominque wasn't surprised that Samson had a boyfriend because she knew that already. The real shocker was who his boyfriend was. Trying to get around that wall as fast as she could, she almost broke her neck, but she dared not let them leave before she could see this with her own eyes.

They were just about to exit when Samson yelled goodbye and at the same time Dominique spoke.

"ANDRE?" Dominique screeched.

Turning around, Andre looked at her like he was about to release everything he had eaten in the last year. He looked that sick.

"You know my bae NiNi?" Samson asked her looking confused.

Samson called Dominique by her nickname when he told Andre to come and pick him up from his friend's shop earlier. Since Andre didn't know any of her personal business, he never knew that she was a salon owner. Had he known that NiNi was indeed Dominique from the church, he wouldn't have been caught dead going there.

At the same time they were having their staring match, Najir walked in. He noticed the way everyone was looking at one another as he walked over to stand beside Dominique.

"What's going on?" he asked. The tension was so thick that it was going to take more than a knife to cut it.

"Samson was just leaving with his boyfriend Andre, that's all," Dominique said clearly amused at the way Najir was looking.

His eyes were all bugged out and his mouth was wide open.

"So this is why you are always bothering my girl. Talking about her and her past, trying to make her feel bad, so you can feel good about what it is you're doing. You are pathetic and I see why she never wanted anything to do with you," Najir said shaking his head.

"What?" Samson wanted to know. He was at a complete loss for words.

"Nah, it's cool, I already had that anyway and it was trash. Maybe it would have been better if you had been alert enough to throw it back. I guess I put too much in your drink that night," Andre threw out there and immediately regretted it as soon as it came out of his mouth.

Dominique, Najir, and Samson already knew what Andre meant. He was the one that raped Dominique all those years ago. He had wanted her for so long and she was never interested so he took it. After that night, it made him madder and madder when she didn't even recognize him. In some sick way, he had hoped that she would remember him, even if it was in a bad way.

Before anyone could react, both Najir *and* Samson were all over Andre throwing blow after blow, while Dominique stood there frozen. If you didn't know by the attire Samson was wearing or the fact that he was gay, you would never know by the way he was fighting. He was in straight beast mode assisting Najir with inflicting as much pain as they could.

Dominique didn't know when the police arrived or who called them until they burst through the door to start breaking everything up. They handcuffed all of the men and separated them so that they could find out what was going on. One thing they knew was that they had someone badly beaten and they needed to get him some help.

The female officer went over to Dominique when she noticed how upset she was, and asked her what was going on. Some kind of way she was able to tell them about Andre and how it all transpired. The officer walked over to the other two police that were there and updated them. One made a phone call and after a few short minutes, they were taking the cuffs off of Najir and Samson.

It took no time at all for Najir to reach Dominique and pull her close to him. He felt her as she shook in his arms, and held her tighter. Because her uncle and aunt made her fill out a police report the night the rape happened, the officer was able to call in and get someone to validate that story. Once she found it to be true, although they didn't have all of the evidence right then, they still arrested Andre because he had confessed.

Finally, that nightmare that had haunted her all of those years was now over, and she could move on with her life. It had always bothered her that she didn't remember too much from that night, but now God had given her the peace that she needed.

This revelation let her know that now she was finally able to give Najir nothing but her best, because in some way she felt like she had gotten her life back together.

Epilogue

The moon cast a glow on the ocean as the waves beat against the shore. There was nothing more peaceful than the sound of the ocean at night and looking out on to the water. It amazed Santana that God could create something so beautiful.

As she stood out on the balcony, she felt the strong arms wrap around her midsection and rub her protruding belly.

"Those two little people in there just can't be still, can they?" Cortez asked as she laid her head back against her husband's chest.

"Don't look for anymore after this because I'm done. It feels like they are wrestling in here."

"That's what little boys do. But I don't know about you not doing this again. I need me a little princess to spoil too," he smiled.

Santana couldn't believe that this was her life right now. Two years ago, if someone would have told her that she and Cortez would have been married and having twins in a couple of months, she would have rebuked them for lying.

When she left town the day after seeing Cortez at the hospital, she didn't tell anyone she was leaving. All calls were ignored, as she spent the first four days in Miami getting in God's face. She needed answers and she knew the only way she would get them was if she went before Him.

On that fifth day, she finally decided to turn her phone back on to what felt like a million texts and voicemails. She had everyone worried and assured them that she was fine. Once she explained to them her reason for leaving, they eased off of her. They knew what she was dealing with and they understood. As long as she was okay, so were they.

The only two people that knew where she was were her parents. Not even her friends knew where she was. If they did, there was no way that they would tell Cortez if he decided to ask. Santana wasn't sure if he would even bother to ask, but just to be on the safe side, she didn't tell them.

So imagine her surprise when fifteen minutes after she hung up with her father while eating lunch, Cortez sat down in front of her. Santana could have sworn she was dreaming and even pinched herself to make sure. When he saw that he chuckled.

"You're wide awake, Tana," he said. Just his voice alone comforted her and she realized just how bad she missed and needed him.

"What are you doing here?" she asked not sure what the answer would be.

"I came to apologize. I fumbled your heart once and if you let me, I promise I won't do it again."

"How did you know where to find me?" Santana asked.

"Pops told me. You know he loves me. Since you didn't tell your little motor mouth buddies, I knew that you would tell your parents," Cortez let her know.

"They can't hold nothing," she said, shaking her head and smiling.

"After you left the other day and granny ripped me a new one, I understood what went wrong. She made me look at what you did in another perspective and through her, God revealed to me that you were the blessing that I had prayed for this whole time. Not just for the money, but to love me unconditionally. The whole time I was calling you selfish, I was being the same way, only thinking of me."

"I'm sorry that I didn't take into consideration if you would be upset or not. Never did I think about how what I did could make you feel less of a man. You needed to do that for yourself and I stepped in.

Cortez, the last thing that I wanted to do was to make you feel like you weren't a man. Whatever you need me to do to help or not help, I'm willing to do. I miss you," Santana said reaching for his hand.

Grabbing her hand, he looked into her eyes. He went on to tell her who Marissa was because he felt like he owed her that too. Never did he want her to ever question his commitment or loyalty to her. And since he didn't officially break up with her, he didn't need her thinking that he had cheated.

Letting go of her hand, he stood up and walked over to her side of the table. He let her know that her bill was already taken care of and to come with him. They walked hand in hand, in what felt like decades since the last time they had been this close to one another.

The restaurant was right on the beach and as soon as they crossed the street and walked down the short flight of stairs that led to the water, that was when she saw what looked like lights flickering on the sand. The closer they walked, the clearer it became and that was when she noticed the flickering was coming from candles in the form of a cross.

Santana thought that was so creative and thoughtful because most times you would see candles or rose petals shaped like hearts. Even if she wanted to, she couldn't stop her emotions from boiling over.

Taking her eyes off of the beautiful sight was when she noticed that Cortez was down on one knee with a beautiful princess cut diamond in a red velvet box.

"All I want to do is love you forever. Will you give me that opportunity and be my wife Santana?" he asked as he cried a tear of his own.

"God knows I will," she said as he slipped the ring on her finger and picked her up in the air.

"As long as I live, I will never make you question why I won't love you, ever again."

***

Now here they were enjoying their two-year anniversary in the same place they got engaged. In the beginning, things were a little rough but they made sure to stick it out. Cortez had opened up the shop that he wanted and business was booming. Things were so good that he had to hire more people and expand the shop. Everything had finally lined up for them and they could credit no one but God.

Kajuana and Michael had grown so much during that time. They had a beautiful year and a half old son who kept them on their toes. Once Michael started working with Najir at his construction company, he was finally back in that head space that he was in prior to his mess up. Kajuana couldn't have been happier and that was all that Michael wanted. Life for them was good.

After the altercation with Andre in her shop, Dominique was all in for her man. Seeing him defend her the way that he did, let her know that he would be the one that covers her whole family. He helped her through the lengthy trial and sentencing of Andre because he knew that she would need him more than ever. When it was all said and done, she felt completely free and there was no better feeling in the world.

Najir loved everything about Dominique and her children, and wanted to make things official. Because she didn't know who Tricey's father was, he decided to adopt her and give her his last name. That was only after he had given it to Dominique first. They had recently celebrated their own one-year anniversary a short while ago and not even three weeks later, they found out that she was pregnant as well.

If there was anything that each of them had a better understanding about, it was that no matter who loved them or not, God did and they would never have to question His faithfulness.

The End

WHY WON'T HE LOVE ME?

For God so loved the world that he gave His only begotten son and whosoever shall call upon His name shall be saved.

John 3:16

Looking for a publishing home?

Royalty Publishing House, Where the Royals reside, is accepting submissions for writers in the urban fiction genre. If you're interested, submit the first 3-4 chapters with your synopsis to submissions@royaltypublishinghouse.com.

Check out our website for more information: www.royaltypublishinghouse.com.

Be sure to LIKE our Royalty Publishing House page on Facebook

CPSIA information can be obtained at www.ICGtesting.com
Printed in the USA
LVOW10s0011160416

483815LV00025B/516/P